As an angel sent to help a struggling soul, getting kidnapped isn't even a blip on Zylen's radar. Before he can connect with Howard, the human he's sent to help, he's taken hostage. He's rescued by the Four Horsemen of the Apocalypse. Zylen recuperates in the Horseman of Pestilence's realm, sharing everything he knows, before continuing on his mission. Finally meeting Howard, he experiences something he never has before — attraction. At first, he thinks it's a by-product of spending time in the demon realm. Then Zylen has an epiphany. Howard is his *stella guida* — his guiding star — the only human in existence whose life would give him more purpose than his duty to his creator. Zylen knows he can't reveal his true nature unless Howard chooses him. Unfortunately, the whole reason he was sent to Howard was to offer guidance as he struggles with a choice — find a girl to date, appeasing his mother, or finally come out. From what Zylen's angelic gifts have shown him, the odds aren't stacked in the *coming out* category. Between meddling family, homophobic females, and the threat of hunters, can Zylen show Howard what can be between them without revealing his true nature and damning them both?

A Little Angelic Interference
Copyright © 2020 Charlie Richards
ISBN: 978-1-4874-2965-2
Cover art by Angela Waters

Published by eXtasy Books Inc or
Devine Destinies, an imprint of eXtasy Books Inc

Look for us online at:
www.eXtasybooks.com or www.devinedestinies.com

A Little Angelic Interference
A Loving Nip: Book Twenty-One

By

Charlie Richards

DEDICATION

There are no negatives in life, only challenges to overcome that will make you stronger.
~Eric Bates

CHAPTER ONE

"How are you feeling?"

Zylen turned upon hearing the melodious tenor. Spotting Pestilence to his left and a smidge behind him, he dipped his head in welcome. "I am well. Thank you, Horseman."

With his hands clasped behind his back, the pale-featured Horseman of the Apocalypse offered a small smile. "You may call me Pestilence, Zylen. I wouldn't mind."

Sighing deeply, Zylen shoved his hands into the pockets of his jeans. "I know this. I apologize for my formality, Pestilence."

The habit was ingrained and difficult to break, even after spending five days in Pestilence's demon realm. He'd been there recuperating from the drugs the human hunters had pumped into his system to keep him sedated. It took a lot to knock out the standard paranormal and even more for Zylen's kind—an angel.

When Zylen had been charged by his creator to search the thoughts of a man named Howard Burnside and offer him a helping hand in choosing the next direction for his life, he'd left his own realm to enter the human one. He'd materialized in a secluded glen north of town. At the same time, he'd put a glamour over his appearance, hiding his angelic aura and large wings covered in feathers of various shades of brown. He'd also clothed himself in a dark gray tank top, cargo shorts, and sandals. It was hot that time of year in Virginia, after all.

1

Before he'd had a chance to track down the human, someone had shot him with a dart. Zylen had been shocked and turned to see three humans in black t-shirts and camo fatigues standing there. All of them had a side-arm attached to their hip as well as some other larger type of gun in their hands, which had turned out to be dart guns.

"Shit, he's not goin' down," the one on the left had muttered.

The guy on the right responded by lifting his rifle and shooting at him again. A second dart pierced his pectoral.

In hindsight, Zylen realized he should have returned to his own realm. It would have been simple to do. Instead, he stood there gaping at the men as his mind grew fuzzy, and he swayed on his feet.

Shock could do that to a being, even one as powerful as him.

The fourth dart had finally felled Zylen, and he didn't remember much after that.

"Do you intend to leave soon?" Pestilence asked, cutting into Zylen's thoughts. "I see you staring at the mists."

Zylen nodded. "I'm nearly back to my full strength, and I have neglected my duties for far too long already."

The mists were used to leave the demon realm, allowing the minions of the horsemen to travel to the human realm. Zylen had paused at the top of the knoll and stared, unable to get his feet to move him closer. His stomach remained in knots, and bile filled the back of his throat.

Unease and shame flooded him at his weakness.

"And yet you linger." Pestilence reached over and rested one fine-boned hand on Zylen's shoulder and squeezed. "Do you wish to talk about why?"

"How did those men know I was not human?" Zylen mused, frowning. "And how could they know where I was going to appear? What if they show up again?"

Zylen had learned from Pestilence that he'd been asleep for two days after being rescued. It had taken another day for whatever he'd been pumped full of to clear enough for him to rise. He'd been weak and uncoordinated, and he hadn't been able to reach his magick until the fourth day.

It had been . . . disconcerting, to say the least.

"We are still searching for answers," Pestilence replied, squeezing his shoulder once more before releasing him. "But I believe part of it is due to witches helping them. Casting spells to monitor ripples in the ether and along lei lines." Shaking his head, Pestilence's expression turned pained. "As for you being caught, that was an unfortunate instance of you being in the wrong place at the wrong time."

As much as Zylen hated to admit it, he figured Pestilence was right. "Which would explain why they were so confused as to why one or two darts didn't take me down."

"Right." Pestilence nodded, his long silky-looking pale hair sliding over his shoulders. "Now you know what to look for and can be on your guard."

"Indeed."

Pestilence smirked, his thin lips curving. "We sent a message to your creator so he could give other angels warning."

Zylen barked a laugh, unable to help himself. "You and your brethren sent a demon to the creator's realm?"

"Several, actually." Pestilence grinned broadly as he waggled his pale eyebrows. "The ripples it created were . . . entertaining."

Imagining that, Zylen chuckled softly. "I bet."

Demons and angels did not traditionally travel in the same circles. Getting in and out of each other's realms required a lot of power. It would involve the combined efforts of all four horsemen to send a demon to the angel realm, just as it would require substantial preparation for the creator to send an angel to the demon realm.

3

Zylen had been an exception, since he'd been brought by the horsemen themselves.

The Four Horsemen of the Apocalypse each had their own crew of demons that worked under them. Just as the demons traveled to the human realm to help balance nature, the angels did the same to balance humanity in a different capacity — emotionally and spiritually.

Judging by the fact that humans threatened paranormals, Zylen thought perhaps they were not doing their job quite as well as they'd thought. Otherwise, why was there so much rampant hate and prejudice? There needed to be more love, understanding, and acceptance.

Which means I better get my rear in gear and go see my charge.

"I will remain vigilant from now on," Zylen murmured. Snapping his attention back to Pestilence, he dipped his head once more. "I am grateful. Thank you."

Pestilence nodded back. "War thinks a great battle is on the horizon, but we're doing our best to hold it back." Lifting his hand, he pointed down the hill, drawing Zylen's attention to two approaching demons. "This is Lucha and Wisner. They will be in your neck of the woods for the next few days. Holler if you need assistance."

"My thanks again, Pestilence."

Zylen turned and eyed the approaching males. Both were tall — although a couple of inches shy of Zylen's own six-foot-six height — with pale features, white-blond hair, and silver-gray eyes. Considering their well-developed wings and stature, Zylen guessed both were upward of eight hundred years in age or more. Young demons did not have wings and appeared more orangutan in form.

"I'm Lucha," the one with longer hair stated.

The slightly shorter demon tapped his own chest. "Wisner."

Offering both a nod of greeting, Zylen stated, "Honored."

Both demons bowed slightly before their master before

4

heading toward the mists.

Zylen followed them.

Mentally tugging on lei lines, Zylen figured out where he needed to go, and between one thought and the next, he returned to the human realm.

The muggy heat immediately wrapped around Zylen, so he once again transformed his clothes. This time he mentally conjured black cargo shorts, running shoes and socks, and a light polo shirt. He felt grateful that by forming his clothing directly on his body, he didn't have to worry about fitting his wings through slits or tears in the cloth. They were already there.

"Good journey to you, Angel," Lucha stated from his left.

"And to you both as well," Zylen replied.

Then the three went their separate ways.

Zylen casted a mental web, searching for the signature of the man he needed to insert himself into the life of—Howard. He found it to the south and headed that way. Another thought had his wings and aura hidden—otherwise, he would be pretty much irresistible to humans.

Angels were beautiful creatures, after all.

So how did the humans who captured me not want to touch and please me?

Another thing Zylen didn't currently have an answer for.

Zylen used his mental abilities to keep track of the humans around him as he strode through town. He caught fleeting thoughts, most of them benign. No way did he wish to be caught unaware again.

A man was reminding himself to pick up milk on the way home. Another planned to call his wife during lunch. A woman wondered why her boyfriend never sent her flowers.

When Zylen heard a man think, *if I catch that fag alone again, I'm gonna teach him a lesson*, he paused and turned. He spotted the human—an athletic-looking dark-haired male.

This is the kind of hatred we need to counter.

Even though it wasn't part of Zylen's task, he couldn't just leave it. He headed toward the man who was crossing a parking lot, obviously heading to his truck. As the guy brushed past Zylen, he skimmed his fingertips over the back of the man's hand.

In that instant, Zylen planted thoughts of acceptance, of tolerance. He even pushed a little indifference in there, too, since he felt a whole lot of anger and disgust. The man's views had been ingrained in him by his father, Zylen learned from his memories.

Zylen saw it often, unfortunately.

The man spun and frowned at him, registering his fleeting touch. Considering Zylen had four inches and plenty of muscle on the man, it was all he did, though. After a grumble about watching where he was going, the dark-haired man continued to his truck.

Moving on, Zylen found the store where he felt Howard's mental signature — some kind of lumber or building chain store. He entered, turning just a little so his wings didn't hit a lady exiting the store. While they were invisible, they were still there, tucked close against his back. For the most part, someone would think they'd brushed against silk and forget about it, but it was still personal to the angel.

Striding down one aisle and up another, Zylen searched for Howard. He spotted him at the far wall, looking at lumber. The human must have sensed his presence, for he glanced Zylen's way, then froze, his eyes widening just a little.

To Zylen's shock, his breath caught in his chest, and he nearly stumbled. The man before him, peering at him with a slightly tired-looking hazel-eyed gaze, was absolutely breathtaking. Big and broad with muscles on clear display under his short-sleeved shirt, he had swirling tattoos up both forearms. His head was shaved, as was his jaw.

Best of all, he stood about six-foot-one and would fit perfectly against Zylen's larger frame.

Wait. Did I just think that? And why is my dick getting hard?

As an angel, Zylen didn't have a sex drive. His body was built for battle, both physically and mentally. He certainly shouldn't be wondering what it would feel like to slide his palms over Howard's scalp or what his skin would taste like when he traced his tattoos.

Did my time in the demon realm change me in some way?

But surely that couldn't be possible. An angel's nature couldn't be altered in any way.

What if the humans' drugs did something to me?

That was a much more likely possibility.

Then Howard yanked his gaze away from Zylen, and he felt it like a physical ache in his chest. He wanted the man's focus back on him so very badly. It felt like an almost visceral need.

Oh my goodness!

That was when it hit Zylen.

This man is my stella guida—my guiding star—a human who will give my life purpose beyond the creator's tasks.

Zylen had heard the rumors, whispered on occasion. To his knowledge, it had been over three centuries since an angel had found his *stella guida*. The angel was supposedly living in Italy, although he'd never tried to confirm that.

God, that man is hot. Howard's thought flittered through Zylen's mind. Another followed quickly. *Damn it. Stop thinkin' like that. I can't be gay. Momma would never understand.*

Remembering his task, Zylen just managed to bite back his wince. The whole point of him being there was to help Howard accept his sexuality. Being gay, straight, bi, or whatever didn't matter. Humans and paranormals alike were made in the creator's image, and it was them who'd come up with the prejudices.

And it looks like he's leaning toward denial.

Please, creator, don't let me be too late.

CHAPTER TWO

Clearing his throat, Howard Burnside returned his attention to the lumber he'd been staring at.

How many do I need again?

Howard groaned under his breath. He'd always been a sucker for big men. The one time he'd gotten up the courage to go to a gay bar a couple of towns over, he'd discovered he had a type.

Standing at six-foot-one and being big and broad due to working out and his physically demanding job as a plumber — toilets, tubs, and pipes were heavy — Howard had plenty of muscle. Couple that with the tattoos adorning his body, and he'd realized he was a twink magnet. Too bad they didn't do anything for him.

Howard's eye had strayed to men even bigger than himself. Unfortunately, none of them had given him the time of day. Since his dick had been hard, he'd taken one of the twinks up on their offer of a back alley blowjob. Howard had jacked off the twink in response.

That had been the one and only time Howard had given in to his base instinct. After that, his own right hand worked just fine. He used the excuse of work and remodeling his old house as an excuse to avoid dating any time his mother asked.

Except that ain't gonna work no more. Goddamn Sunday supper with some girl.

"Excuse me. Howard, isn't it?"

The deep voice sent a wash of tingles down Howard's spine. He turned toward the speaker and discovered it was

9

the big, hot guy.

He's speaking to me, and he knows my name.

That was . . . unexpected.

Howard had to swallow twice to get enough moisture into his throat so he could reply. "Y-Yeah?"

Great. Could I sound any more inane?

He tried again. "Yes, I'm Howard." That was better. "Do I know you?"

'Cause I'm pretty sure I'd remember meeting someone like you.

The man grinned widely, which only made him look even more stunning. "No, we've never met, but your reputation precedes you." He held out his hand. "I'm Zylen."

Acting on instinct, Howard took the man's hand. "Zylen. Unusual name." His face heated when he realized what he'd just blurted out. Clearing his throat, he muttered, "Sorry."

"I hear that a lot. Don't worry about it."

Howard nodded, and that was when he realized Zylen continued to grip his hand. His palm was warm and dry, and the contact caused the fine hairs on his arm to stand on end. When Howard made a move to release the man, Zylen tightened his hold just a little.

"I have something I'd like to speak to you about," Zylen claimed. "Can I buy you a cup of coffee?"

This man wants to buy me coffee? What the hell?

Even though his attraction to the guy made him dangerous, Howard couldn't resist.

"Sure. When?"

"Now, if you have time," Zylen told him.

Howard really didn't. He barely had enough time to get the lumber unloaded at his house that he was going to use to frame the new bathroom space before he had to clean up, change, and get to his mother's for Sunday supper. Except, he really didn't want to go, and being late would mean less time in the company of whoever she'd invited.

"It would have to be a short chat," Howard told him. "I'm

expected somewhere in a little bit."

Zylen nodded. "Tell you what. How about we hit one of those drive-thru coffee kiosks on your way to your house, and I'll help you unload this. That way you won't be too late?" Rubbing his thumb over the back of Howard's hand, Zylen sent tingles up his arm as he continued, "We'll chat in your truck and beyond."

Dropping his focus to their still-clasped hands, Howard sucked in a sharp breath. He could see goose bumps on his flesh. His gut clenched, and his cock throbbed.

Being in close proximity to this man was such a bad idea. "Okay."

"Thank you, Howard."

Just the way Zylen said his name sent a zing down his spine.

Holy shit!

After a few more caresses and a squeeze, Zylen released his hand.

Howard immediately wished he could take it again. He wondered what it would be like to be able to twine his fingers with Zylen's. Would the bigger man allow it? He'd held onto his hand an awfully long time.

That's an indicator of interest, isn't it?

Zylen eased a step closer, putting him right up into Howard's personal space. Then he bent a little, dipping his head.

For an instant, Howard thought Zylen was going to kiss him . . . right there in the store. His breathing hitched, and his heart pounded. His pulse raced through his veins, and blood roared in his ears.

"Howard, choose the wood you need for framing your new bathroom."

Zylen whispered the words into his ear. His breath was warm on his skin. A shiver worked down his neck.

"H-How did y-you—" Howard began to ask, but his voice failed him.

"Would you like me to get a cart for you?" Zylen asked, still too close. "Give you a second to pull yourself together, *stella guida?*"

Howard finally took a step back even as he turned his head. Zylen's lips were *right there*.

"Great creator, but the way you look at me," Zylen whispered huskily. "We really need to get out of here so we can talk."

"T-Talk," Howard croaked. "Right."

"I'll be right back." Zylen touched Howard's forearm, skimming his fingertips down it. "Don't go anywhere."

After another couple of seconds, Zylen pivoted and strode away.

Unable to help himself, Howard roved his gaze all over Zylen's retreating form. The muscles of his tall, broad frame were on clear display under his shorts, and the polo shirt clung to his wide shoulders. His shaggy light-brown hair hung in waves to his nape, and Howard's fingers twitched with his desire to bury them in it.

And that ass! Holy fuck!

Howard's dick ached, releasing a bead of pre-cum.

Then Zylen turned down an aisle and disappeared from view.

As if some spell had been broken, Howard finally blinked. He sucked in a ragged gasp, then swung around to face the lumber. After a quick glance around, confirming that he was alone, he reached down and adjusted his dick.

"What the hell was that," Howard muttered to himself. Resting his right hand against a rack holding two-by-sixes, he panted heavily. "I should so run." Instead, Howard rubbed his left hand over his shaved scalp and waited for Zylen's return.

While Zylen wasn't gone long, only a minute or two, it was long enough for Howard to calm his racing pulse. He also thought about the dinner with his mother that evening, which killed his raging boner. Feeling a bit more in control, he pulled out the slip of paper he'd written his numbers on and began choosing his lumber.

Well, Howard thought he'd gotten himself under control, until he spotted Zylen striding toward him. Even partially hidden behind the lumber dolly, he still found him to be a gorgeous specimen of manly perfection. His sun-kissed tanned skin almost appeared to glow.

And who has aqua-colored eyes? Are they contacts?

"Here we go," Zylen stated with a grin. "How many do you need and which sizes?"

During the next few minutes, Howard and Zylen worked together to fill the trolley. Zylen asked about his house project, and Howard answered. He explained about how he'd bought a dilapidated home in a nice neighborhood. It had stood empty for a number of years, so timbers were sagging, windows had been boarded up, and rodents had made nests in it.

Still, the bones of the structure had been solid, so while the four-bedroom, two-and-a-half-bath home with a turret was a bit bigger than he'd originally planned to buy, he'd fallen in love with it. The fact that it had a detached three-car garage had helped him make the decision, too.

"It sounds amazing, Howard," Zylen told him. "I can't wait to see it."

They chatted all through check out, crossing the parking lot, loading up his truck, then to the coffee kiosk. Never once did it get awkward or uncomfortable. They didn't run out of things to say. After chatting about the house, Zylen began asking him about his interests — work and hobbies.

Sometime between getting their coffee and driving to his house, Howard realized it felt like a date.

Oh, holy fuck.

Tension threaded up his neck.

After casting a quick look Zylen's way, Howard tightened

his grip on the steering wheel. "What am I doing here with you?"

"We're getting to know each other," Zylen replied with a smile. Reaching over, he rested his big, warm hand on the back of Howard's neck and massaged lightly. "It's what people who are interested in each other do, Howard."

"I'm not gay," Howard blurted out, louder than he'd intended. "I can't be."

Zylen hummed, but he didn't remove his hand. "Can or can't, we both know you are." His voice rumbled through the truck's cab, deep and soothing. "The chemistry between us is . . . undeniable, Howard. I felt it the instant our eyes connected."

Howard swallowed hard, trembles working down his spine, created by the exquisite feel of Zylen's hand. "I-I . . ." He took a deep breath, then let it out slowly. When he managed to get the lump out of his throat, he tried again. "Zylen, this isn't . . . I can't—" Howard snapped his mouth shut. He had no idea what he was trying to say.

Turning in his seat, Zylen didn't seem to have that problem. "I'm not going to lie. I knew who you were when I followed you into that store, Howard. I wanted to meet you." He continued to massage him. "I feared you were having trouble with your sexuality and thought perhaps you needed someone to talk to. Someone impartial." Zylen sighed deeply as he leaned closer. "I'm not so impartial anymore, I'm afraid. Now I'm invested."

Howard's mind scrambled. He tried to unravel everything Zylen had just said. "H-How'd you know who I was?" Stopped at a red light, he looked at the man. "Who told you about me?"

When Zylen had told him that his reputation preceded him, Howard had immediately assumed it was his reputation as a plumber. He realized now it was something else. Except, that didn't make much sense.

"I've never told anyone that I check out guys."

Except that one time at the club, but I didn't give that guy my name. Was there someone there who knew me? Someone I didn't notice?

Zylen tipped his head and narrowed his stunning aqua eyes just a little. "No one needed to tell me. It's the way you look at people, I think."

"Shit," Howard hissed.

A car horn honked, and Howard realized the light had turned green. He started them moving again.

"Don't worry, Howard." Zylen released the back of his neck and straightened. "It's very subtle. Only someone looking for it would notice."

Howard wasn't certain if that made him feel better or — "Wait. You were looking for it? Why?"

Zylen winked. "Because of our chemistry."

"How long have you been watching me?"

While Zylen didn't give off a creepy stalker vibe, maybe Howard was wrong.

Is it really a good idea to take him home with me?

"Please relax, *stella guida*," Zylen rumbled. "You are always safe with me."

Before Howard could question the odd nickname — that was the second time Zylen had used it — the other man continued.

"And I have not been watching you long. I came to town a while ago, then had to leave again." Zylen grimaced. "Not my choice, but things happen."

For the first time, Howard saw uncertainty in Zylen's expression. It made him want to reassure him, but he didn't understand why. Instead, he stayed silent.

"May I ask why you think your mother won't understand? Has she made homophobic remarks to you?"

Once again, Howard's heart began to race but for a new

reason.

"How the hell do you always seem to know what I'm thinkin'?"

CHAPTER THREE

Oh, dear. I'll definitely have to be more careful.

As an angel, picking up other's thoughts was second nature. Humans, however, did not have that ability. Once Howard bonded with him, he would develop the gift.

Dear creator, how can I convince him?

Zylen had never tried to woo someone in his life.

"Well?"

Hearing Howard's harsh demand, Zylen thought quickly. He never wanted to lie to his *stella guida*, but he couldn't tell the man he was an angel, either. There were rules to follow. First, Howard had to accept his sexuality. Then he needed to choose Zylen. He had to say the words.

"I'm sorry," Zylen began slowly, half turning in his seat once more. "You have a very expressive face at times."

Howard did, too—his eyes were troubled, his brows furrowed, and his lips tense. Zylen wanted to kiss him and help him ease those lines. He'd barely restrained himself in the store, but once they were at Howard's home, Zylen had no intention of controlling himself.

Over the years, Zylen had heard that kissing was even more intimate than sex, not that he'd done either.

"Many mothers try to find a nice girl for their son, so they are taken care of. I've seen it many times," Zylen continued, choosing his words carefully. "Is it your father who is homophobic?"

Howard nibbled his bottom lip, and the uncertainty on the big man's face made him appear all the more endearing.

17

Zylen wanted to lean over and capture that plump bit of flesh between his own teeth. His desire to taste almost felt like a living thing within him.

Zylen's concern grew when Howard didn't respond. As he'd been around for thousands of years, he had patience. He relaxed in the seat and waited.

When Howard had pulled his truck into a driveway, Zylen took in the structure that appeared through the trees. He whistled softly. The home appeared exactly as Howard had described — old, run-down, with a turret, and a lot of charm.

What Howard had failed to share was the fact that the home was shaded by large willows and other trees, obstructing the home from any neighbors' views.

Excellent.

Howard turned his truck around in the large loop driveway, then backed up to the garage. After he shut off the vehicle, he turned his attention back to Zylen.

Once more, Zylen waited, openly perusing the man, admiring his features.

"My father passed away when I was eight. Skin cancer," Howard told him. "I don't remember him too well."

"I'm very sorry to hear that," Zylen replied truthfully.

Howard shook his head. "It was a long time ago."

Zylen opened his mouth, then closed it again.

"My sister is older by three years. Her name's Lilibeth," Howard told him. "She's married now to Macon. He's real good to her. They tried to have kids for years, but it never happened. After a battery of tests" —his hands tightened around the steering, his knuckles turning white, betraying his emotion just as easily as the strain in his voice —"they found out she's sterile."

"By the creator." Zylen felt his gut clench with sadness. "Your family has been through quite a bit."

Howard nodded. "Right." He stared straight out the window. "So how can I tell 'em I'm gay and put them through even more shit?"

Zylen couldn't resist. Reaching over, he placed his hand on Howard's thigh. He felt the tensing of the hard muscle beneath his palm, even through the fabric, as he heard Howard suck in a harsh gasp.

"I am confused," Zylen admitted, keeping his voice soft, soothing. "How is you admitting your needs to your family putting your family through more . . . stuff?"

Perhaps it was his choice of word, for Howard focused on him. He arched one brow and smirked at him. "Stuff?"

Yup. Definitely my word choice.

"I don't make it a habit to cuss, Howard." Zylen shrugged one shoulder. He didn't mind his *stella guida* teasing him. It helped lighten the mood. "Wouldn't your family want you happy?"

"Well, sure," Howard replied, his amusement slipping. "But my mom wants grandkids."

"Ah." Zylen nodded slowly. "Of course."

Zylen wondered what Howard would say if he knew that he could correct Lilibeth's problem. One touch from him, and she would be made whole. Of course, that would require meeting his human's family.

And I can't tell him until after he accepts me.

Catch twenty-two.

However . . .

"There is surrogacy," Zylen pointed out. "It is extremely common these days."

Howard's brows furrowed. "Huh."

At least he appeared to be thinking about it.

"Let's get this lumber unloaded." Zylen offered him a chance to think without pressure. "I understand you have somewhere to be."

Zylen managed to keep the fact that he knew Howard was being set up that evening out of his words. His human hadn't told him, after all. He'd just thought it.

Nodding, Howard pushed out of the truck.

Zylen immediately missed the feel of his thigh beneath his palm.

While Howard opened the garage, Zylen put down the tailgate. He drew out several boards and carried them inside. Pausing in the spacious room, he peered at all the equipment that indicated Howard's job as a plumber.

Howard walked past him, carrying a couple of boards of his own.

Following, Zylen stacked what he held where Howard did.

Together, they made short work of unloading the truck.

"The number of boards you carry at a time is impressive." Howard eyed the four two-by-sixes Zylen grasped. "Were you a bodybuilder at some point?"

Zylen shook his head. He could have carried more, but he knew that would have appeared suspicious. He grinned.

"No, but it pleases me that I impress you," Zylen admitted, sweeping his gaze over Howard as they moved past each other. "I enjoy watching your muscles bunch and release beneath your skin as well."

A board slipped from Howard's hand, nearly landing on his foot. "Jee-suz!" he cried, jumping back.

Zylen was there in an instant, catching the falling board. He steadied it, so it wouldn't hit Howard on the arm as it toppled. With one hand on the board, Zylen placed the other on Howard's hip. His thumb slid under his shirt, grazing warm, firm flesh.

In an instant, Zylen's dick roared from half-mast to full and aching. His skin prickled, and he couldn't fight his soft moan. He skimmed his palm up a little, pushing under the fabric, needing more.

"Z-Zylen?" Howard rasped.

Meeting Howard's gaze, Zylen peered into his *stella guida's* wide eyes. His hazel orbs were heavily dilated—the green dominating. He had his lips parted, and he panted softly.

As Zylen watched, Howard swept his tongue along the bottom of his plump flesh.

"Howard."

Zylen breathed his human's name as he lowered his head. Having never kissed before, when his lips were a hairsbreadth from Howard's, he hesitated. To his undeniable pleasure, his *stella guida* closed the scant distance.

The first press of Howard's mouth against his own nearly made Zylen forget himself. His glamour flickered as his magick surged. Fortunately, Howard had his eyes closed.

Regaining just a little control, Zylen put it back in place. He pressed a bit harder against Howard's lips as he slid his tongue along his bottom lip. While Zylen had never done it, he'd seen others kiss, and he wanted inside Howard's mouth.

How to make it happen?

To Zylen's relief, Howard's lips parted.

Zylen eased his tongue into Howard's mouth. When he slid his own along his human's, the man's flavor burst across his tongue. There were hints of coffee, cream, and something else — something masculine and rich.

Something all Howard.

Finding the man delicious in a way Zylen had never experienced, he tightened his hold on his hip. He tilted his head a little as he delved deeper. His tongue lapped at Howard's mouth as he explored and feasted.

Zylen felt his erection throb in time with his heartbeat, twitching with an insistence he'd never felt before. Instinctively answering the call for pressure, he eased closer to Howard. Needing his other hand free, needing more, everything, Zylen broke the kiss.

With ease, Zylen tossed the board in the direction of the other wood. Then he grabbed the two from a clearly shell-shocked Howard's grasp and threw them, too. They landed with a clatter on the concrete floor, but Howard didn't look away from Zylen's gaze.

Moving his newly empty hand to Howard's waist, Zylen gripped his hips. He lifted his human easily, drawing a shocked cry from him. As Zylen began walking toward the workbench five feet away, Howard wrapped his arms and legs around him.

"Holy shit, you're strong," Howard commented between his panting breaths.

"Uh-huh," Zylen confirmed absently as he placed Howard on the bench. Then he slid his right hand to his rear as he moved his left up to cradle his nape. Pushing forward as he pulled tight, Zylen flushed their bodies together.

When Zylen felt Howard's equally hard erection slotted against his own, he cried out with pleasure. Howard's answering moan was music to his ears. Rocking his hips, Zylen peered into Howard's flushed face, taking him all in.

Howard's tight grip on his shoulders registered just as Zylen sealed his mouth over his human's again. His senses sang with bliss as heat twisted in his belly. He ravished the man as his body coiled tighter and tighter.

Zylen suddenly felt on the precipice of . . . something. A harsh shudder racked him, and uncertainty bloomed within him. He broke the kiss as a noise he'd never made before escaped his throat.

The press of Howard's long legs around his waist, keeping them locked together, continued the pressure on his dick. Howard clung to him, rocking . . . rocking. Suddenly, as if a dam had burst, his *stella guida* cried his name.

Stars burst across Zylen's vision.

His groin flashed hot.

Then . . . ecstasy.

Zylen trembled in Howard's hold, clutching his human against him, as he flew on the wings of his first orgasm.

They could have stayed like that forever, and Zylen

wouldn't have cared. He reveled in the experience they'd just shared. His human had torn him asunder and put him back together even as he'd done the same to him.

Pure bliss.

"Wow," Howard finally mumbled, lifting his head from where he'd had it pressed against his neck. "Never felt anything like that."

A wash of pride slammed into Zylen. He lifted his own head and grinned down at Howard.

"Me either," Zylen admitted. Sliding his palm up Howard's neck, he satisfied his curiosity and massaged the human's scalp. "Smooth."

Howard smiled. "I just shaved it yesterday."

"May I ask why you shave it?" Zylen couldn't contain his curiosity, especially with the residual traces of pleasure loosening his control over his tongue.

"Premature gray and balding runs in my family," Howard admitted. His lips quirked up a little at the edges. "Guess I'm a little vain."

"You are gorgeous any way you look, *stella guida*," Zylen replied, enjoying the touching.

"What's that mean?" Howard cocked his head. "*Stella guida*. You've called me that a few times."

First, Zylen carefully corrected the pronunciation, then explained, "Guiding star. You are my guiding star." Having to be honest, he admitted, "If you accept my claim on you, I will follow you anywhere, give you anything, and live my life to please you."

Howard's lips parted, and his eyebrows shot up. "Wow." He cleared his throat. "You don't mess around."

Not understanding, Zylen tipped his head. "Mess around?"

"Yeah," Howard replied, nodding. "Ya just lay it all out there. Very blunt."

"Oh." Zylen licked his lip as he thought quickly. "I suppose, I believe honesty between us is key."

With his cheeks a little pink, Howard rubbed his hands over Zylen's shoulders. "Well, uh, okay." Then he smiled as he squinted up at him. "Your eyes really are aqua-colored, aren't they? At first, I thought it was contacts."

"No contacts," Zylen confirmed. "Really aqua."

"Huh. Unique, like your name."

Actually, all angels had varying shades of aqua-colored eyes, but Zylen couldn't tell him that.

Howard eased back, resting a hand on the workbench he sat on. "Damn." Peering down between them. "Can't believe I came in my pants like a horny teenager."

Zylen didn't completely understand the reference, but he nodded anyway. They had come in their pants, after all. He had just never been a teenager.

Grinning back at him, Howard opened his mouth . . . but the ring of a phone interrupted them.

Howard groaned as he pulled his phone off his belt. "Shit!"

Zylen spotted the word *Mom* on the screen before Howard swiped it, answering, and he knew that, for now, his time was up.

CHAPTER FOUR

Dinner at his mother's was the last place Howard wanted to go after experiencing the most intense orgasm of his life. Even the expert blowjob from the twink at the club hadn't made him rocket off that hard. He couldn't help but wonder — if frotting and kissing Zylen created those sensations, what would actual fucking feel like?

And god, from the feel of his erection pressing against mine, not to mention the size of the big man, I bet Zylen is hung like a horse.

Could I actually take something that size up my ass?

Howard had toys.

Who didn't?

But none of his dildos and plugs were even close to what he'd been rubbing his erection against.

Pulling up to the home he'd been raised in, Howard heaved a tired sigh. He would much rather have taken Zylen up to the house, enjoyed a leisurely shower together, then a nap. Instead, he was going to be fielding questions from his mother, whoever she was setting him up to meet, and doing his best not to think about the amazing man who was waiting at home for him.

Okay. So maybe he's not amazing. I don't know that, yet. I do know I want to find out.

Just listening to Zylen's voice and hearing his blunt declarations made Howard's heart rate spike in his chest. That was how attraction was supposed to feel. He knew that.

And I'll never have it with a woman.

How could that be fair to her?

Goddamnit!

Pushing his round-robin thoughts out of his mind, Howard exited his truck. He hustled up the drive, eager to get in the house and out of the muggy Virginia heat. Even though he wore nice shorts and a light polo, Howard still felt himself start to sweat.

Of course, it was entirely possible that his sweating was caused by what he was about to face.

Howard had never knocked on his childhood home's door, so he just grabbed the knob and turned. It opened, and he stepped inside. After closing the door, he toed off his sneakers.

"Hey, Ma!" Howard hollered. "Sorry I'm late." He headed down the hall toward the dining room. "I got caught up at the—"

"We're in here still, Howie."

Hearing his mother's voice to the right, Howard paused where he was passing the arched opening that led to the front salon. He panned his gaze over the group clustered in the room. His gut clenched as he took in the situation.

Lilibeth sat with Macon on one of the small love seats. Another was occupied by Macon's best friend—Benjamin, who'd been the best man at his wedding—as well as his wife, Samantha. His mother—Tiffany—sat near one end of the long sofa in the room. Near the other end sat Shirley, Samantha's younger sister. All of them held drinks in their hands.

Good grief. They haven't even started dinner, yet.

Pasting on his best smile, Howard entered the room.

Shoulda kept my shoes on in case I need to run.

"Hi, everyone. Sorry I'm late," Howard repeated as he crossed to his mother. He gave her a hug and a kiss on the cheek, then headed to Lilibeth. As he bent and hugged her, too, a little harder than necessary, he muttered, "I'm going to kill you later."

Lilibeth knew that Howard didn't care for Shirley. Not one

bit. How Samantha could be so kind and sweet while Shirley came out an entitled drama queen, Howard would never know.

"Sorry," Lilibeth squeaked back.

Howard didn't buy it. His sister could have at least warned him. Instead, he hadn't been given any heads up that he should have taken an uber instead of his truck.

Oh well. At least I have something to look forward to at home.

Crossing to the sideboard, Howard grabbed a crystal decanter filled with whiskey. "Does anyone need anything while I'm up?"

After filling drink orders where Howard took the time to drink his entire first glass, he heeded his mother's repeated urgings to join her and Shirley on the sofa. With his second glass in hand, he obeyed. In between the two women, he did his best to stay closer to his mother without being too obvious about it.

"So, what's everyone up to these days?" Howard asked casually, turning his focus on Benjamin. "You still at Warton and Rydel?"

Last Howard had heard, Benjamin was on the fast track to becoming a partner at the firm where he worked.

"I am," Benjamin confirmed, grinning, relaxing on the sofa. "And Samantha is hosting a fundraiser for the cancer ward at the hospital. We wanted to give you your invitation personally." As Benjamin spoke, Samantha pulled an envelope from her purse. His expression turned stern, yet still playful. "You ducked out of the last two, but this time there's a bachelor auction, and we're putting you up on the chopping block, big fella."

Even as Samantha passed the invite to his mother, who in turn, put in on his lap, Howard groaned. "You asshole," he growled, glaring at Benjamin, who was now laughing.

"Language, Howie," his mother gasped, as if she'd never heard a curse in her life.

Right.

Still—"Sorry, Ma," Howard immediately replied.

Howard really did like Benjamin. For being a fancy lawyer, he'd always remained pretty down-to-earth. Still, he sometimes pulled ridiculous shenanigans.

"Come on, man," Macon cut in, leaning forward. "We all had to volunteer someone. Nedrick is going to be up there, too."

"Well, at least I'll have someone to commiserate with," Howard grumbled before taking another sip of his drink.

Nedrick was Macon's little brother. At six-foot-even with a lithe runner's build and sun-kissed skin, he was a very handsome man. He bet the guy would bring in a good price.

He was also a womanizer and a cad, and Howard was wondering when he would grow up. At least he was fun to talk to.

"I bet you didn't have to twist his arm very much," Howard commented.

Macon chortled, proving Howard right.

"Well, I think you'll bring in top dollar, Howie," Shirley purred, sliding closer and resting her hand on his thigh. "I know I'll be bidding on you."

Unlike Zylen's touch on his thigh in the truck, which had caused heat and tingles and a coil of need to flair in his gut, Shirley's touch left Howard feeling dirty . . . as if he needed to go shower.

Plus—"I'd appreciate it if you'd call me Howard, please, Shirley," he corrected. He barely tolerated his mother calling him that. Holding her gaze, Howard forced a smile. "Thank you."

Shrugging one shoulder dismissively, Shirley slid even closer. "So, Bennie told me he offered you a position at his firm."

Bennie?

Howard noticed Benjamin grimace.

"When are you starting there?" Shirley pressed.

"Really?" His mother sounded surprised, so obviously she hadn't heard about it either. "That's amazing, dear! I didn't know you were going to take up law again." She gripped his forearm and squeezed. "I'm so happy for you."

At least that explained why Shirley was all over him. No way would the blonde want a plumber for a husband.

Turning his attention to his mother, Howard forced a smile. "Actually, while Benjamin did offer to get me a placement there, I turned him down." Even though seeing her crestfallen look hurt, he could never go back there. "I love what I do, Ma. I'm happy."

After working his way through law school, because it'd been expected of him since his late father had been a lawyer, Howard had decided it wasn't for him. He hated working inside, not to mention the politics. Howard loved working with his hands as well as owning his own business.

His mother let out a small sigh before patting his cheek lightly. "Well, that's all any mother wants for their child." Her smile appeared a little forced, but at least she was smiling. "I'm glad you're happy."

Would she be glad if Zylen was sitting next to me, holding my hand?

The thought came out of the blue, and just the idea of sharing Zylen with his family caused a strange mix of desire and nerves to swirl through his gut.

As Howard took another sip of his drink, Shirley eased away from him.

Thank god.

"Oh, you know who else will be up on the block?" Macon cut in with a grin. "Cross."

Howard didn't know who that was.

"Leland Cross?" Benjamin asked, clarifying. After Macon nodded, Benjamin told everyone, "He's a new attorney at our firm."

Just as Shirley leaned forward and said, "Really?" Benjamin continued, "What would he know about going on a date with a woman? He's gay."

Howard felt as if his heart skipped a beat in his chest. His stomach knotted, and his grip on his tumbler tightened. To his surprise, Macon laughed while reaching over to slap Benjamin's arm.

"He doesn't have to sleep with whoever buys him. This is for a date, not to crawl into bed with the guy." Macon continued to chuckle as he shook his head. "I bet the ladies will flock to him because they won't feel pressured for more than a nice time." Then Macon waggled his brows. "Besides, maybe some hot stud will win the bid."

To Howard's surprise, Benjamin nodded. So did his wife and Lilibeth. None of them seemed to care one iota that this Cross guy was gay.

Could I have been reading things wrong?

"Ugh, that's disgusting," Shirley grumbled, tossing her long blonde hair over her shoulder. "How can you joke about something so perverse?"

Benjamin frowned as Macon sobered.

"What do we care who someone else shares their bed with," Samantha commented quietly, perhaps trying to smooth over her sister's nonsense. "Love is love, right?"

"No, it certainly isn't," Shirley snapped. Turning her attention to our mother, she was obviously looking for support in that corner. "Surely you agree that two men together is sinful and wrong."

When one heartbeat passed, then two, Howard felt his throat dry up. He took a drink of whiskey.

"Well," his mother began. "I can't say as I understand why a man would want to enjoy the company of another man that way, but it's not my place to say." She hesitated another instant, then added, "I certainly wouldn't want someone to come into my home and tell me what I can and can't do with someone I love, so what right do I have to say that about someone else?"

Well, damn.

That was a diplomatic answer.

Howard's head spun, and he didn't think it was from the alcohol with no food. His family didn't give a shit about gay people. He had to wonder if that would change if he came out to them.

It would, wouldn't it?

While in theory, knowing some random person was gay was completely different than having a brother or son or father who was gay.

Right?

Maybe not.

Shirley gasped, sounding truly scandalized. "Why, Misses Burnside. I never would have thought you were a fag-lover." She leaned away from us as her gaze landed on Howard. "Surely a big strong man like you wouldn't condone such illicit behavior."

Howard lifted his whiskey to his lips and took a sip. At the same time, he remembered the heat and pleasure and all-consuming need he'd enjoyed with Zylen as they'd shared moments of *illicit behavior*. His heart rate skyrocketed just thinking about it.

After lowering his glass, Howard met Shirley's gaze squarely. "I don't know why you think I would support your views." He smirked at her. "After all, I'm gay."

Then Howard finished his drink.

Shirley screeched and jumped to her feet. Her face red, she slapped him across the face just as he lowered his empty tumbler.

Good thing he'd already swallowed.

Chaos ensued as everyone jumped from their seats and began shouting.

Howard slowly rose before crossing to the sideboard.

He fixed himself another drink.

CHAPTER FIVE

The rumble of the engine coming up the driveway did *not* belong to Howard's truck. After riding in it only once and listening to it drive away, Zylen already knew the sound. Peering out the downstairs window, keeping to the shadows of the dimly lit room, he watched the vehicle come into view.

Zylen had appreciated the fact that Howard had invited him to stay. He knew it was partly due to the bond already forming between them. While he hadn't tasted his human's seed or blood, they'd exchanged enough saliva to get it started.

Can't wait for the chance to complete us.

While the vehicle was a truck, it was a *Ford* instead of a *Dodge*. The model appeared newer than Howard's. Even in the dark, his keen eyesight let him see that it didn't have the dings and small scratches associated with a working man's truck.

Zylen glanced at the clock, noting it was quarter til eleven. Howard had told him he hoped to be back by nine-thirty. He would have worried, but through their tentative bond, he didn't sense any true distress.

The truck stopped directly in front of the porch steps. When the engine cut out, the quiet chirping of crickets returned. The driver's side door opened, and Zylen watched a dark-haired man step out.

"You can stay here, honey," the man said as the passenger door began opening. "I can get him inside."

"Oh, no," she countered. Then a blonde appeared, sliding

33

from the truck. "It'll be easier if I help. I'll get the door while you get Howard out."

The man bobbed his head in a nod of acknowledgment, then opened the door behind his own.

The woman headed around the truck's hood and began climbing the stairs.

Zylen figured he had about ten seconds to make a decision. He could cloak himself in an invisibility spell. Then they would never even know he was there. On the other hand, he didn't know these people, and they were about to enter Howard's home.

Watching the man ease Howard from the back seat of the quad cab, Zylen cocked his head. His *stella guida* leaned heavily on the guy. Howard's left arm had been pulled around the man's shoulders, and the stranger gripped it for leverage while keeping his other arm around Howard's waist. The man staggered under Howard's much heavier frame as he struggled toward the house.

Decision made.

Even as the front door began swinging open, Zylen flipped on the front room's overhead light.

The woman gasped, staring up at Zylen with her mouth gaping, and fear filled her hazel eyes.

Oh my god! I'm gonna die! Someone's robbing my brother's house.

Zylen heard the woman's stray thought and realized how it could look that way. It also told him who the people were—family. Howard had told Zylen he had one sister—Lilibeth—and she was married to a man named Macon.

These have to be them.

"Hello, Lilibeth," Zylen greeted, keeping his voice low and soothing. "Looks like Macon is having a tough time with Howard. Let me slip on past you, and I'll give him a hand."

Lilibeth's eyes somehow managed to get even wider, but

she obeyed. The instinct was a natural one for humans. Sometimes, being an angel came in handy.

Zylen fought back a smile.

It's always handy.

Once Lilibeth eased sideways, Zylen strode past her.

Who the hell is this?

Zylen heard Lilibeth's mental question, but she held her tongue. He figured that wouldn't last long. Macon, on the other hand, he was not silent.

When Zylen came striding out of the house, his gaze snapped from where he'd been focusing on the steps. His eyes narrowed, and his jaw tightened. He looked beyond Zylen, obviously checking to see if he could see his wife.

"Who the fuck are you?" Macon demanded. He tightened his grip on Howard as he took a step backward. "What are you doing here?"

"My name is Zylen," he told Macon, offering him a small smile. "Let me help you with Howard."

Zylen didn't give the man a chance to disagree. He bent and slid one arm around Howard's back, causing his human's dangling arm to ease over his shoulder. Then Zylen slid his other hand under his knees and easily hefted his *stella guida* into his arms bridal style.

The tightness in his chest eased. It took every bit of self-control he had not to nuzzle his cheek across Howard's shaved scalp or to kiss his forehead. Instead, he breathed deeply . . . and smelled a wide range of things—mostly alcohol and perfume, but there were still hints of Howard's cum from when they'd fooled around earlier.

My man needs a shower. Too bad he's in no condition to take one.

Turning, Zylen headed back up the steps and into the house.

"Hey, I asked you a question," Macon snapped, following. "What the hell are you doing here?"

Zylen struggled with how to answer that without outing

Howard.

Holy shit! If I had a man like this waiting at home, I'd want my family to know I was gay, too.

Hearing Lilibeth's thought, Zylen nearly tripped on the carpet runner. He caught himself just in time, then peered over his shoulder at the pair. Lilibeth continued to stare with wide eyes, while Macon scowled.

Zylen opened his mouth, trying to process what he'd just heard.

Did Howard come out, and that's why he's three sheets to the wind? Had it or had it not gone well?

Howard took that second to rouse slightly. Lifting his head, he stared up at Zylen through glassy eyes. A wide smile curved his lips.

"Hey, Zylen," Howard slurred. "You stayed."

"Yeah, I stayed, *stella guida*," Zylen murmured softly. "Anything you ask. You know that."

"Thanks."

When Howard sighed deeply, his whiskey-coated breath wafted across his face, and Zylen grimaced. "Let's get you to the bathroom, so you can clean up."

"I'll find his *Tylenol* and get him a bottle of water while you do that." Lilibeth closed the front door. "Come on, Macon. Give me a hand."

"Wait," Macon began, but Lilibeth shushed him.

"It'll be so much easier for Howard's boyfriend to carry him up to bed." As Lilibeth pulled Macon past him, she waved her hand up and down his frame. "I mean, look at that. He's not even breaking a sweat. We were just gonna dump him on the sofa."

While Macon continued to frown, he followed his wife deeper into the home.

Zylen climbed the stairs with ease. He'd explored the house briefly after Howard had left, then spent most of his evening meditating in the screened-in porch out back. The master bedroom had been easy to find.

"Howard?" Zylen jostled his human gently. "Howard, wake up for a minute."

Howard opened his eyelids to half-mast and stared up at him with a crooked smile. If he hadn't been drunk as a skunk, it would have been a sexy look.

Smiling back at Howard, Zylen ordered, "I'm helping you brush your teeth. Then I'll strip you to your underwear, wipe you down a little, and pour you into bed. Got it?"

"Okay," Howard whispered. "Sorry about this."

"It's okay. We'll talk about what happened tomorrow."

Howard repeated his okay.

Zylen flipped on the bathroom light with his elbow before easing Howard to his feet. He kept his arm around his waist, since his human was none-too-steady. Then he helped him brush his teeth. Zylen smiled at the domesticity of it.

Of course, Zylen figured Howard would probably be embarrassed the next day, but he would get over it. This was what partners did for each other. After Lilibeth's comments — both spoken and unspoken — Zylen prayed that was the direction they were headed.

Once the tooth brushing was finished, Zylen left Howard for a moment to pee. He heard a thud, a grunt, and a curse through the door, so let himself back in. Seeing Howard leaning heavily on the sink, his pants and underwear around his ankles, and his eyes closed, Zylen shook his head.

At least he got it in the bowl . . . mostly.

Zylen pulled Howard's underwear up but removed his pants. Then he undid several buttons of his shirt before pulling it and the undershirt over his head. Finally, he took a damp hand towel and wiped it over his face, neck, and pits. He used the same towel to wipe the stray drops off the toilet bowl.

Leaving everything on the floor, Zylen once again lifted Howard and returned to the bedroom. He tucked him into bed and drew the covers over him. Unable to help himself, he pressed a kiss to Howard's forehead.

A throat clearing drew Zylen's attention, and he straightened, finding both Lilibeth and Macon standing in the doorway. Macon appeared a little uncomfortable, but Lilibeth was smiling.

Huh.

Lilibeth came forward and held out a small bottle that contained pills as well as the water bottle.

Zylen hesitated. He wasn't entirely certain what they were for. When she wiggled them a little, he took them. Figuring Howard would understand when he woke, Zylen placed them on the nightstand.

Guess I'll need to learn human ways.

Macon cleared his throat again, once more drawing Zylen's attention.

Lilibeth beckoned.

Curious about what would happen, Zylen followed them out of the room.

Lilibeth led him and Macon into the kitchen. Turning, she held out her hand. "I'm Lilibeth. Howard's sister."

Zylen took it and shook. "Zylen."

After releasing her, Lilibeth cocked her head. "But you already knew that, didn't you?"

"I did."

Waving at Macon, Lilibeth continued, "And you know this is Macon, my husband."

While Macon still remained the warier, he went through the process of shaking Zylen's hand.

Such an odd custom.

"How long have you and my brother . . . um" — Lilibeth waved her hand a little in apparent confusion — "been together?"

Zylen hoped to get away with being slightly vague. "We

have not known each other long. We are still . . . working toward a relationship." If things went sideways with Howard's family, Zylen figured he could get one of the demons to alter their memories. "Your brother is worth the wait."

"Is it because Howard was in the closet?" Macon asked from where he leaned against the counter. "He came out tonight, ya know."

"Partly."

A very small part.

"He feared how we'd respond," Lilibeth acknowledged sagely. "We'd never really talked about homosexuality at home. It just . . . never came up."

"Until tonight." Macon snickered.

Zylen figured there was a story there. He would wait and ask Howard tomorrow. If he asked them, they would continue to linger, and Zylen wished for them to go. All he wanted to do was slip into bed with Howard and wrap his arms and wings around him.

"So, we'll be seeing more of you, then?" Lilibeth cocked her head. "You said you didn't know him long, but you're here in his house. Are you living together?"

Shaking his head, Zylen smiled at her. "Howard asked me to stay so we could talk after he returned."

"So you just . . . stayed?" Macon sounded confused.

Zylen shrugged. "Yes."

It really was just as simple as that.

"Ooookay," Macon muttered.

Lilibeth bumped her shoulder against her husband's, then grabbed his hand. "Well, we'll let you take care of him, then." She tugged Macon toward the arch that led back toward the front door. "He's gonna be pretty hungover, in pain, and maybe a little embarrassed. Don't let him drive you away because of it. You seem like a decent fella."

Zylen nodded, accepting her advice, although she didn't know him from Adam. He knew her easy acceptance was tied into the whole angel aura, not that she would know that.

"Nice to meet you," Lilibeth called over her shoulder.

Then they were gone.

After locking the door behind them, Zylen turned off lights before heading back upstairs. He undressed, using magick to remove his shirt, since getting it around his wings was tough. As Zylen eased into bed beside Howard and tucked him against his side, the idea of taking away his pain so he wouldn't be hungover occurred to him.

Zylen didn't do it, though, for two reasons. One—people needed to learn from their actions. Two—it would be incredibly difficult to explain without giving away Zylen's nature.

Chapter Six

Howard would have groaned, but that would have made the pounding in his head even worse. Instead, he whimpered softly as he struggled to pull a few thoughts together. Slow and steady, he recalled the previous evening.

Well, most of it.

Prying open an eyelid, Howard squinted, taking in the furniture before him. He recognized his nightstand and dresser. The door to his ensuite bathroom stood open, and there were clothes and a towel on the floor.

How did I get home?

Then a large warm hand slid over his hip, causing him to freeze.

"Relax, Howard." Zylen's deep voice rumbled from behind him. "How are you feeling?"

Suddenly, the warmth blanketing him made sense.

Zylen is in bed with me.

When had that happened?

Did we fuck?

Howard forced his body to relax, more because tensing his shoulders just increased the ice pick stabbing his brain with every beat of his heart. Plus, the way Zylen's hand rubbed over his chest felt really nice. Even his cock was taking notice, thickening — which was covered by underwear.

So we probably didn't do anything.

"Like I got hit by a truck," Howard rasped, forcing himself to answer Zylen's question. Then he spotted the bottle of *Tylenol* and water on his nightstand. "Oh, thank god."

41

Reaching over, Howard hated the tremble in his hand. He grabbed both items but couldn't get his fingers to coordinate enough to open the pill bottle. Moaning in frustration only made his head hurt worse.

The heat drew away from his back as Zylen shifted on the bed. "Here." He took the bottle and opened it easily. "How many?"

"Four."

Zylen didn't question him, merely slid that many onto Howard's palm. Then he replaced the cap before grabbing the water bottle. He opened that, too, then carefully held it to Howard's lips after Howard had popped the pills into his mouth.

After swallowing several gulps, Howard paused. His mouth still tasted like shit, and his tongue felt thick and fuzzy. Unfortunately, his stomach was roiling, and he really wanted to keep the pills down.

Howard felt himself being eased toward his back a little. Opening his eyelids, which he didn't remember closing, he didn't fight the movement. He found himself being draped over Zylen's warm torso while the other man sat against the headboard and held him.

It felt . . . really nice.

Also, for some reason, the way Zylen massaged his temple eased his headache faster than anything had . . . ever. It wasn't gone by any means, but he no longer felt like he was going to hurl any second. Even the tremble in his limbs ceased.

"Never again," Howard whispered.

Zylen chuckled softly. "I have heard those words many times over the years."

Scoffing hurt when Howard did it on instinct. "Yeah," he muttered, believing the big man. "What are you doing here?"

"Taking care of you."

Howard smiled upon hearing Zylen's simple and honest answer. "Thank you."

"You're welcome, Howard." Zylen's muscle under his cheek moved a little before he felt the man kiss his temple. "Feeling better?"

"Quite a bit, yeah," Howard admitted. Furrowing his brows, he asked, "Do you know how I got home? I was gonna call an uber."

"Lilibeth and Macon delivered you to my care."

Howard's grip where he was resting his arm around Zylen's waist tightened. "You met 'em?"

"I did."

Well, holy fuck.

"They appreciated me being able to carry you up the stairs."

Howard snapped his head up, which made him wince from renewed pain. Still, he asked, "You carried me up the stairs? Seriously?"

Zylen held his gaze with his oddly amazing aqua eyes. "I did." He traced his fingertips over the light rasp of Howard's morning stubble. "I would not lie to you." Holding up the water bottle, Zylen asked, "More? Or are you ready to rise? I hear eating eggs and toast helps, too."

Choosing the water because Howard didn't want to get up quite yet, he took a few sips of the offered bottle. Then he laid his head back on Zylen's chest. The other man hummed, relaxed under him, so Howard decided he must not mind.

"You heard eggs and toast helps?" Howard questioned softly, not wanting to break the intimacy. It felt too good.

"I did."

"Never used the technique yourself?"

Zylen shrugged a little under him. "Never needed to."

"Really?" Howard turned his head and met Zylen's gaze again. "Never been hungover?"

Shaking his head, Zylen stated, "I have not."

"Doesn't swear. Has never drank too much." Howard returned his cheek to Zylen's pectoral. "Helped me when I was sloshed. Even managed to get my overprotective sister to leave me with a complete stranger." That one stumped him a little. "How'd you manage that?"

"You came out to your family last night," Zylen stated, although that wasn't an answer.

"Yep." Howard still couldn't believe he'd done that. The words had just sort of ... exploded out of him. "The guys were talking about a gay coworker, and Shirley started insulting him, and they backed the guy. I just—" Howard shook his head a little, unable to explain.

"That was nice of them." Zylen rubbed his other hand up and down the curve of Howard's spine as he continued to massage his temple with the other. "I believe Lilibeth thinks we have been dating for a while. I ... may have misled her a little to draw that conclusion. Sorry."

Howard hummed softly, then let out a sigh. "Don't be. This is ... really nice."

"It is," Zylen agreed.

Taking a chance, Howard murmured, "I think I could get real used to it." When he felt Zylen's hands pause, he quickly added, "Not the you caring for me when I lose my shit and drink too much, but this part ... the holding, uh, that ..." Howard floundered.

Shit!

Zylen's arms shifted and tightened, pressing Howard closer to him. "Me, too, *stella guida*," he rumbled. "Me, too."

Howard began to smile. He had to admit that Zylen's pet name was growing on him.

"I—" Then Howard spotted the time on his alarm clock. "Fuuuuuck," he snarled as he pushed away from Zylen. "I didn't set my damn alarm."

Zylen released him, glancing from the time on the clock to Howard's face. "What is it?"

"I'm supposed to be at the Benson place to work on plumbing in ten minutes," Howard told him as he slid off the bed. His head swam a little, and he gripped the mattress to steady himself. "I gotta call Jack and tell 'im I'm running behind."

"I will prepare the eggs and toast while you call and clean up."

Just that fast, Zylen offered to help. "And your truck is still at your mother's," he reminded him, drawing another cuss from him. Zylen shook his head with a smile. "I'll drive you over there."

Howard started toward the bathroom. "You have a truck? When did you grab that?"

"It's a *Jeep*," Zylen told him, heading out of the room. "I picked it up while you were at dinner last night." Then he disappeared out the door.

Shaking his head, amazement filling him, Howard turned on the shower. He shucked his underwear as he returned to the bedroom. His phone was on the nightstand, so he made his call while the water warmed.

"You better not be calling in sick, Howard," Jack said by way of greeting, a growl in his voice.

Howard couldn't help but smile. While Jack could be a bastard to work for sometimes, he was a good man who appreciated Howard's work. He was also meticulous and detail-oriented. Jack had turned out to be a pretty good friend after eight years of working together.

"I'm not," Howard assured. "I'm just running a smidge behind. I'll be there in an hour."

Jack heaved a deep sigh through the line. "Good."

Cocking his head, Howard couldn't help but ask, "Everything okay? You sound sorta stressed."

"Misses Benson changed her mind on the cabinets again."

Howard cringed, feeling sympathy for Jack. "Damn. Sorry, man."

Jack had agreed to renovate most of the main floor of the Benson's home. That included the kitchen, dining, and living space, as well as a powder room, an office, laundry room, and master suite. The floor plan Misses Benson requested would open the space up to give the older home an open concept.

Unfortunately, getting Misses Benson to choose her kitchen cabinets was problematic. One day she wanted everything all white. The next day she preferred earth tones. She needed to make up her damn mind, since everything else in the home was going to be based off them.

"Did you tell her the order for the white ones was already placed?" Howard asked as he squeezed toothpaste on his brush.

"'Course I did," Jack groused. "Hey, is that the shower? Did you just get up?"

Howard sighed, but he wasn't going to lie to the man. "Yeah, sorry. I forgot to set my alarm. Had a mandatory Sunday supper with my family and, uh, it sorta got out of hand."

"Out of hand, how? Wait, wait." Jack backtracked. "Tell me when ya get here. Hurry up." Then the line disconnected.

Chuckling, Howard brushed his teeth.

A couple of minutes later, as Howard showered, he realized he didn't feel nearly as shitty as he should, especially considering how much pain he'd been in when he'd cracked his eyelids.

Huh.

After getting dressed, Howard found a meal of bacon, eggs, hashbrowns, and toast waiting for him in the kitchen. Zylen was also already dressed and ready to go. He had no idea how the big man had managed it, but he appreciated it none-the-less.

"I don't have time to eat all this, but it sure looks amazing," Howard admitted. "Thank you."

Zylen grabbed a piece of toast, then layered some of the eggs, bacon, and hashbrowns on it, topping it with a second piece of toast. With a wink, he took a piece of parchment paper—*I didn't know I had any of that*—and wrapped it around the quickly fashioned breakfast sandwich. Finally, Zylen handed it to him.

"We'll eat on the go," Zylen told him as he made a second sandwich for himself. Then he handed an open thermos of coffee to Howard. "You added a dash of cream at the coffee shop, but all you had in the fridge was half-and-half. I added a bit of that. Did I get it right?"

Howard took a quick sip and hummed appreciatively, impressed. "Perfect, thanks."

Wow. He noticed how I take my coffee.

"Come on." Zylen picked up another travel mug, obviously one for himself, and led the way toward the front.

Bemused at how Zylen had completely made himself at home, Howard followed. He couldn't say he minded. In fact, if he was being honest with himself, he liked it a lot.

It couldn't be this easy though, right?

Why not, though?

Howard had never been in a relationship before. He'd seen his sister date and get her heart broken several times before Macon had come along. Her experiences had made him leery of ever trying anything. Of course, there was also the issue of his sexuality.

No one had fit . . . until now.

Wanting to find out more about the man who'd just swept into his life, Howard climbed into the passenger side of the *Jeep* and tried to decide what to ask.

As Zylen started the open-topped older model vehicle—traditional green with roll bars—Howard asked, "So, Zylen. Where are you from?"

To Howard's surprise, Zylen froze. He slowly turned his head until he was caught in the man's aqua-colored gaze. His jaw tightened a little as he swallowed hard enough to cause his Adam's apple to bob.

"A long way away," Zylen murmured, concern radiating in his expression. "I could take you someday, if you wanted to go, but we couldn't stay there. I . . . I can't go back permanently." Reaching over, Zylen squeezed Howard's hand. "My place is with you."

Then Zylen returned his hand to the steering wheel and got them moving.

As Howard ate his sandwich—occasionally giving directions so Zylen knew where to go, he watched Zylen do the same. With one hand he held his breakfast. With the other, he not only handled the stick shift, but he also steered the wheel.

It was really impressive, and sort of breathtaking with his multicolored brown hair blowing in the wind.

Finishing his food, Howard realized Zylen had given him the strangest non-answer.

The man had not told him where he was from, only that he planned to stay with Howard.

It made Howard's heart race in a really nice way.

Except, it all sounded too good to be true—a kind, considerate, sexy man arrived right when he needed him?

There has to be a catch, right?

CHAPTER SEVEN

When Howard had woken in so much pain that Zylen could practically feel it radiating off him, he hadn't been able to help himself. While he hadn't taken all the ache away, he had eased it considerably. Zylen's nature to care for his *stella guida* demanded it.

Currently, Zylen was driving his magickally created *Jeep*, following Howard's instructions to return him to his own truck so that the man could go to work.

Zylen would prefer to stay by Howard's side until their bond was complete. He just wasn't certain how to make that happen. If he asked to join him at his work, would that be odd?

His answer to Howard's simple question of, *where are you from*, was strange enough.

Wasn't it?

It wasn't as if Zylen could tell Howard, "I'm from the realm inhabited by angels formed by the creator."

Howard hadn't chosen him yet, even though things seemed to be leaning in that direction. His human had come out to his family, at least. Zylen himself had met Lilibeth and her husband, although that was more by accident. He'd made him breakfast and coffee, and they'd shared a meal together.

Ah. A meal!

"I didn't have time to prepare a lunch for you," Zylen commented as he pulled his *Jeep* to the side of the road behind Howard's truck. "May I bring you a meal at your job site or pick you up so we can go somewhere together?"

49

Howard paused, his coffee in hand, with his other on the door handle. "You don't have to do that."

"But I would like to." Zylen rested his hand on Howard's thigh, squeezing lightly, enjoying the play of muscle jumping beneath his palm. "Please?"

After another heartbeat of hesitation, Howard nodded. "Maybe bring me something? A sandwich or sub? Nothing fancy. It's a construction site, after all," he finished with a wry smile. "Give me your number, and I'll text you the address."

Number. Ah, as in phone number.

Nodding, Zylen reached into the pocket of the driver's side door. With a hum of power, he transformed a notepad into a phone. Since he had no idea what the number attached to it would be, Zylen brought up the texting function as he asked for Howard's number.

Zylen quickly input it into the device, so pleased that he'd kept up with modern technology, even if he normally didn't use it.

That is changing fast.

Then Zylen texted a quick message to Howard.

This is Zylen. I look forward to lunch.

Howard's phone chimed. He opened the message.

Zylen took the opportunity to verify his number and commit it to memory.

With a roguish grin and a sly glance Zylen's way, Howard typed a message back.

Me, too. I'll get back to you soon.

Chuckling under his breath, Zylen couldn't remember when he'd experienced such levity. He responded with, *See that you do.*

Howard laughed, then opened his vehicle door.

Unable to help himself, Zylen reached for the man. He wrapped his hand around Howard's nape and drew him close. Zylen sealed his lips over Howard's.

Howard's gasp of surprise gave Zylen access to his mouth.

He thrust his tongue in deep, tasting coffee, food, and man. After a few seconds, Howard kissed him back, making Zylen's heart rate soar.

When breathing became necessary, Zylen broke the kiss and eased back. He peered at Howard, taking in his dilated pupils, plump lips . . . and shell-shocked expression.

"Howard?" Zylen kept his worry out of his voice, but just barely.

"Y-You just kissed me."

Zylen nodded. "I didn't get a good morning kiss," he pointed out. "I certainly didn't want to miss out on a goodbye kiss, too."

Howard swallowed hard enough to cause his Adam's apple to bob.

Worry flooded Zylen.

Did I just screw up?

"But we're on the street in an open-topped *Jeep*."

Zylen still wasn't following.

"Anyone could have seen," Howard elaborated.

"Ah, I should have asked permission." Zylen released him, straightening in his seat. "Howard, I want you to be mine just as surely as I want to be yours. That will never change, and I don't care who knows it." Seeing the furrowing of Howard's brows, he added, "We have only known each other a day, so how could you trust me, right? How could I know for certain?" Zylen waved his hand to indicate their surroundings. "Wherever we are doesn't matter to me, as long as you are comfortable. I'll do my best not to initiate a kiss in public if that is your wish."

It would be horribly difficult, but Zylen would do his best.

"I've never met someone who shows such certainty, and" — Howard sucked in a deep breath, then let it out slowly between pursed lips — "and I want what you're offering. I'm just . . . worried."

Deciding to go for broke, Zylen asked, "You came out to

51

your family last night, Howard. Do you *choose* me?"

Then Zylen waited with bated breath.

Howard flicked his gaze all over Zylen's face, obviously searching for something.

Zylen could only pray to the creator that Howard found what he was looking for.

Finally, Howard dipped his chin in a slight nod. "Yeah."

The single whispered word caused Zylen's heart to race. Still, he needed something a little bit more. "I need you to say it, please."

For a second, Zylen didn't think Howard would.

A flicker of confusion crossed Howard's face. When it cleared, Howard smirked. "You do like the words, don't you?"

"I find it necessary for clear communication," Zylen countered.

Howard nodded. "Clear communication is necessary for any relationship." Then he grinned. "Zylen, I *choose* you."

A crackle of magick rushed down Zylen's spine, pulling a gasp from his lungs. Goose bumps caused the hairs on his body to lift as a rush of wind surged through the *Jeep*. A low rumbling sounded through the sky.

Snapping his gaze upward, Howard glanced around. "Was that thunder? I didn't think it was supposed to rain today."

Seeing as Howard needed to get to work, Zylen knew he didn't have time to explain, not right then.

Soon.

"Thank you, Howard," Zylen said instead. He squeezed his human's thigh again before offering, "This evening, when we return to your home, I'll explain why I feel so confident in my connection for you already."

And pray for a good outcome, because we've already begun our bond.

Howard nodded. "Sounds good." Then he began easing out of the *Jeep*, but he paused. Turning back, Howard leaned in and pecked a kiss to Zylen's lips. "See you for lunch."

Zylen was too startled to respond, and then Howard was jogging to his truck and climbing in, disappearing from view.

Still, Zylen grinned widely.

After Howard pulled away, Zylen did the same. He returned to his *stella guida*'s home simply because he had nowhere else to go. Settling in to meditate while waiting for Howard's call, Zylen decided to contact his creator and share his news.

Zylen figured the ancient being would have already felt the shift in the dynamic of their relationship, but respect deemed he disclose his good fortune personally, even if through a telepathic bond. No way was Zylen leaving the human realm until he was completely, totally bound to his human.

"Great creator," Zylen began. "Will you speak with me?"

A warm sensation flowed through his mind.

I am here.

"I have found my *stella guida*. We have started our bond."

I have felt it. After a second, the creator continued. *Congratulations, my child.*

"Thank you. He has chosen me."

Yes.

Happiness and pride filled Zylen. "I will share everything with him this evening."

Be careful. There are still hunters in the area.

Zylen nearly snapped his eyes open, which would have severed the connection. Instead, he frowned. "What permission do I have to secure the safety of myself and my *stella guida*?"

There was a long-standing order that angels were never to harm a human unless specifically instructed. Zylen had never had issue with the order before. After encountering the hunters himself, however, he needed guidance.

Any who attempts to harm your stella guida is fair game, my child.

Zylen found that surprising, but it filled him with relief, too.

The creator spoke again before Zylen decided on an acceptable response.

Although it would be better if the action was handled by Lucha and Wisner, so as not to taint the soul of you and your stella guida.

"Of course, ancient one," Zylen replied, nodding absently. It made sense that his creator knew the demons were in the area and that Pestilence had given him the means to contact them. The horseman's touch on the shoulder had linked them, so he could mentally ask for assistance if he needed. "I'll contact them."

Zylen also knew that a tainted angel, depending on the severity, would no longer be able to return to the realm of his creation. Still, if it was a choice between Howard or his home realm, he would gladly give up the ability to visit. He wouldn't end up there much after bonding with his human anyway. A human couldn't stay in the angel realm for any length of time, even if they did have a pure soul.

The place was too . . . *much*, creating lethargy. They would lie down to enjoy the view or the feel of the grass or the wind on their skin. Eventually, they just wouldn't get up again.

The chime of his phone drew him from his thoughts. Once again, he nearly opened his eyes but resisted the temptation. He had one more question.

"Did you know Howard was my star?"

I did. More angels will be interested in spending time in the human realm once they here of this. You will most likely have company.

Zylen couldn't say he was surprised.

Enjoy your eternity, my child.

"Thank you," Zylen whispered, but the warm buzz in his mind was already lifting, telling him the creator had left him. "That sounded suspiciously like a goodbye."

Picking up his phone, Zylen put the oddness out of his

mind. He smiled upon reading the message.

Can you be here around 1PM?

That was followed by an address.

I'll be there. See you soon.

See you, came through a few seconds later, and Zylen couldn't stop grinning. Never in his millennia-long existence had he felt such anticipation. It was . . . thrilling in a way he'd never before experienced.

I have a date with my stella guida.

Using the app on the phone, Zylen mapped the address, seeing how long it would take to get there. Then he searched for a suitable sub shop to get sandwiches. As he did that, a thought struck him, so he sent Howard another text.

Are there others at your job site that will need food?

Zylen waited another five minutes before the response came through. It gave him time to decide where he was going.

Are you offering to buy the crew lunch? Why?

Hesitating an instant, Zylen tried to decide how to respond. Finally, he chose, *because it would be rude to eat in front of someone who doesn't have anything, and because it is just as easy to buy two sandwiches as it is ten.*

Fuck! You're a keeper! There's eight of us here today.

Zylen laughed at Howard's reply as he typed his own.

Sounds good. See you in a bit.

CHAPTER EIGHT

"What has you grinnin' like that?"

Hearing Jack's gruff voice, Howard turned and found him leaning against the ensuite bathroom's door frame. He had his arms crossed over his expansive chest, and a smirk curved his lips. The blond was even doing the eyebrow arch.

Howard cleared his throat, then offered, "Just settin' up lunch for everyone. I know we normally bring them in a pail or head to a nearby taco truck, but, uh, my friend is joining me for lunch, so offered to feed everyone."

Jack's second brow lifted to join the first. "Your friend offered to buy everyone on the job lunch?"

Nodding, Howard felt his cheeks flush a little. "Yeah. He's really nice like that." Lifting his phone, he checked the text again. "It's rude to eat in front of someone who doesn't have anything, and it's just as easy to buy ten sandwiches as two." Howard shrugged. "Or close enough."

"Huh. Awful nice of her." Then Jack's eyes narrowed. "Wait. You said he, didn't you?"

Howard nodded once, barely resisting the urge to bite his lip.

Jack's scrutiny was making him nervous.

"This a date with this guy, Howard?" Jack asked, blunt as always. It was one of the reasons Howard enjoyed working with him. His friend never pulled punches . . . unless it was a client. Then Jack had a little more tact. "This your way of sharin' somethin' with me after eight years?"

Sighing, Howard shoved his phone in his pocket. He lifted

56

his other hand to the back of his neck, rubbing absently.

Scoffing softly, Jack muttered, "Wow. It is." He unwound one arm and pointed at him. "That's your tell. Scratchin' the back of your neck."

"Tell?" Howard immediately lowered his hand. "What the fuck?"

Jack chuckled, fucking *chuckled*! At least he wasn't getting upset. "Aww, I don't give a shit about that. As long as your work is good, you know that. Who ya wanna fuck in your bedroom is your business." Easing away from the frame, Jack righted himself as he waggled his eyebrows. "I'll meet your beau, man. Make sure he's good enough for ya."

Scowling, Howard blurted out, "Kinda the other way around, Jack. He's *too* good for the likes of me." He frowned at the floor as he realized the truth of that. "Not entirely sure what he sees in me."

But we're gonna talk this evening. Maybe it'll be clearer then.

Slapping him on the upper arm, Jack made Howard rock a little. "That can't be right. You're a hard workin' mother-fucker." He wasn't a small man, standing an inch over Howard's six-foot-one height and just as broad and muscled. "Why wouldn't ya be good enough for 'em? And how come ya didn't tell me sooner? Didn't trust me?"

To Howard's surprise, he heard a hint of hurt in Jack's tone. Meeting his friend's gaze, he quickly shook his head. "It wasn't that. I struggled with it a long time." Grimacing, he admitted. "Still do, but he's makin' it a damn sight easier." Thinking of Zylen's kisses, his touch, drew a smile to Howard's face.

Jack laughed. "Ya got it bad, man." He patted him on the shoulder again. "I'm happy for ya."

Got it bad? Since when? I met the man yesterday.

Some of his internal panic must have shown on his face, for Jack tsked. "Aww, don't freak out. It happens to everyone at some point in their life." Then he patted his chest. "Not me, of course, but" — he shrugged and gave him a rakish grin — "most people."

Then Jack turned and started out of the bathroom. He paused and spun, snapping his fingers. "Oh, I actually came over to see if you're still on track to finish this bathroom's plumbing by this evening."

Howard stood in the master ensuite bathroom, putting in all new piping due to the age of the home. After a quick look around, mentally going over everything that still needed to be done, he nodded. "Yup. I got this."

Jack gave him two thumbs up as he grunted, then headed out of the room.

Letting out a deep breath, Howard shook his head.

Wow.

Just like that, Howard knew his professional life would remain on track if he continued to see Zylen.

And since I'd already told him I chose him, that's damn sure what I want.

With that thought in mind, Howard turned back to the pipes.

Howard worked steadily for the next couple of hours, until Dwyer hollered his name.

"Yeah!" Howard shouted back.

"Some guy here to see ya."

Unable to help himself, Howard smiled as he put down the piece of pipe he'd been fitting. He rose to his feet and, as he dusted his hands on his jeans, headed toward the front of the place. Spotting Zylen standing just inside the door, he swept his gaze over the big man.

The sunlight through the opening glinted off the lighter browns in his hair. It looked like highlights, but Howard would bet his bottom dollar that it was all natural. He just didn't think Zylen had a vain bone in his body.

When Zylen's gaze landed on Howard, he smiled warmly.

Howard grinned.

Zylen lifted his arms, drawing Howard's attention to the bags he carried. "I come bearing gifts." There were two plastic sacks in each one of his hands. "I hope I'm not interrupting. I know I'm about fifteen minutes early."

"Not interrupting at all," Howard replied, stopping to stand in front of him. His fingers itched to touch. Realizing that if Zylen had been a woman, Howard wouldn't be fighting his desire, he gave in. "It's good to see you," he murmured huskily as he rested his hands on Zylen's chest. Then he tipped his head back and leaned forward, making his request plain.

"Here?" Zylen whispered, appearing uncertain.

Howard knew Zylen wasn't denying him. Instead, it was the comments they'd shared in the *Jeep* earlier that had him questioning him.

"Here," Howard said with certainty.

Zylen immediately dipped his head and pressed his lips to Howard's. It was really only a soft meeting of lips, a light press. Neither of them deepened the kiss or searched for more.

That didn't stop Howard's heart from racing like a freight train in his chest or for his breath whooshing from his lungs and leaving him lightheaded.

Damn. How does he do that?

"Hi," Howard whispered roughly. "Welcome."

"Hi," Zylen responded, his voice just as low and gruff. "Thank you."

"What the holy fuck?"

Howard released one of Zylen's hips so he could pivot. Spotting Dwyer's incredulous expression, he frowned. "You got somethin' to say, Dwyer?" Howard demanded, deciding to go on the offensive.

"Since when do you kiss dudes?" Dwyer demanded, his voice squeaky, waving his hand toward him and Zylen.

"Since I damn well please." Howard saw no reason to explain himself to the framer.

"Yeah, but—" Dwyer started.

"Hey, what's the problem out here?" Jack rounded the corner and glanced around the room, obviously taking in the situation at a glance. "Oh, hey, man." Jack grinned as he headed toward Howard and Zylen. "Thanks for bringin' lunch. Awful nice of ya." He held out his hand. "I'm Jack, Howard's buddy and partner in crime."

Zylen handed the bags in his right hand to Howard, so he could shake Jack's hand. Glancing inside, he realized they were filled with a number of massive hoagies.

"Partner in crime?" Zylen murmured, clearly questioning as he released Jack's hand. Then he cleared his throat. "I'm Zylen."

"Don't listen to him," Howard grumbled, shaking his head. "I've never done any crimes."

Jack laughed as he rested his hands on his hips. "Just an expression, Zylen." He peered over his shoulder and ordered, "Hey, Dwyer. Round up the guys. Lunch is here."

Dwyer sputtered for a second as he drew closer. "Y-You knew about this? That Howard is a—"

"Careful how you finish that, Dwyer," Jack warned, lifting his hand and pointing at the man. "My company has a firm no discrimination policy. Don't cross it."

His eyes widening, Dwyer nodded. "Yeah, yeah. I, uh, I'm just shocked. Ya know." He waved his hand toward them again. "I mean, look at 'em."

"Homosexuals come in all shapes and sizes," Jack told him on a long-suffering sigh. "You want food or not?"

"Yeah, boss. Did you see the label on the bag?" Dwyer pointed. "That's Minelli's. They make the best hoagies this side of town."

"Well then, you better round everyone up so you can eat

one."

Upon hearing Jack's repeated command, Dwyer bobbed his head and scurried away.

Turning back to them, Jack indicated that they should head outside. Since it was a build site, Zylen shouldn't be inside without a hard hat. If he intended to visit often, Howard would have to get him one.

Jack guided them toward a group of picnic tables. After plopping down on a bench, he sighed deeply. Resting his hands on the table, he asked, "How long have you and Howard been dating?"

Howard placed the bag of sandwiches on the table and shook his head. "No grilling," he ordered, pointing at his friend.

Lifting his hands in placation, Jack just grinned.

"Just long enough for me to realize how amazing Howard is," Zylen replied smoothly, winking at Howard. "This bag contains a number of single-serving chips and such. Let me go get the drinks. They're still in my *Jeep*."

After giving Howard's upper arm a squeeze, Zylen headed toward the street.

"Damn," Jack muttered under his breath, drawing Howard's gaze away from Zylen's amazing ass covered in cargo shorts. "Hoagies, chips, and drinks? He *is* totally too good for you."

Howard dropped onto the bench across from Jack and put his head in his hands. "I know, right?" Feeling a slap on the back of his head, he lifted it and glared at a scowling Jack. "What the fuck was that for?"

"For being a dumbass." Jack snorted, rolling his eyes. "I saw the way he looked at you. He's just as smitten as you are."

"Ya think?" Howard asked, since he couldn't very well deny how infatuated he already was with the man.

Jack nodded as he grabbed a sandwich and began opening

it. "So, really. How long have you been dating him?"

Howard shook his head as he took his own sandwich. They were all labeled, and there were far more than just eight. There had to be a dozen of them.

Opening the roast beef and cheddar sandwich, Howard held up one finger.

Cocking his head, Jack asked, "One date?" He took a bite while Howard shook his head and did the same. "One month? Week?"

Swallowing his food, Howard admitted, "One day."

Jack coughed, his food obviously going down the wrong way.

In an instant, Zylen was there, offering him a red flavored drink of some kind. He even patted his back lightly. Zylen looked at Howard questioningly as Jack got his breath back.

"He asked how long we've been together," Howard told him, seeing no reason to lie. He shrugged. "The answer surprised him."

"Ah. Of course." Zylen rounded the table and settled beside Howard, placing his hand on his thigh. He smiled warmly at him. "Sometimes, you just know."

Howard returned his smile as he bumped his shoulder into Zylen's. Then he returned to eating, choosing a bag of *Harvest Cheddar Sun Chips* to go with his beef and cheddar hoagie. Zylen picked up a pastrami.

Jack sounded a little hoarse when he spoke again, but not too bad. "Well, congrats. I'm happy for you."

Over the course of the next few minutes, the others stopped by the table. They said hello to Zylen and introduced themselves. Most of them were polite, although a few looked a little leery about touching him. One look from Jack corrected that.

They all trickled away with food and drink, settling at other tables, except for Dwyer. He sat next to Jack.

Jack had just swallowed a chip when he snapped his fingers and pointed at Howard. "What are ya gonna do about the bachelor auction?"

"What do you mean?" Howard frowned. He'd forgotten that he'd told Jack about that earlier that morning. "What am I *supposed* to do about it?"

Shrugging, Jack pointed between them. "Is Zylen okay with you being auctioned off to some lady for a date?"

Zylen growled low in his throat, and Howard jerked his gaze to the man. A flush covered the bigger man's cheeks, and his aqua eyes flashed. If the look of anger hadn't been directed at him, Howard would have thought the look was so fucking hot.

"It wasn't my idea, and I didn't sign myself up for it," Howard blurted out.

"Explain," Zylen demanded.

Howard did as swiftly as possible. Seeing the amused expression on Jack's face made him want to deck the guy.

Fortunately, as soon as Howard finished the explanation, Zylen relaxed. "Easy. I'll buy you myself."

Dwyer hooted as Jack chuckled.

Relief filled Howard.

Okay then.

CHAPTER NINE

Zylen still had no idea how he was going to explain the paranormal to Howard. Pacing the back porch, he thrust his fingers through his hair. He scratched at his scalp as he ran through possible scenarios.

Everything sounded ridiculous.

"How the hell do shifters explain mates to their humans?" Zylen grumbled.

"I think I'm a bad influence on you."

Whirling around, Zylen spotted Howard leaning against the doorframe. He hadn't even heard his *stella guida's* truck, nor the squeak of the door hinges. Then the man's words registered.

"What?"

"Bad influence." Howard smirked as he pointed at him. "You just swore."

Sighing deeply, Zylen rested his hands on his hips as he tipped his head back. "I did." He closed his eyes. "Dear creator, forgive me. I am . . . struggling."

"You're not talking to me right now, are you?"

Zylen snapped his eyelids back open and focused on Howard. "No, I was praying to my creator."

"So you're religious." Howard nodded. "That's not a deal-breaker. Is that what you were trying to figure out how to explain?" Then his eyebrows furrowed, and he frowned at Zylen. "What's a shifter?"

Shock flooded Zylen . . . as well as a little hope.

"Where did you learn about shifters?" Zylen moved closer

64

to Howard. "You know of them?"

Howard's eyebrows shot up his forehead. "Uh, no." He pointed at Zylen. "You just used the word." Rubbing his palms over his jeans, he eased away from the door jam. "Zylen, what's going on?"

"Right, I did," Zylen whispered. He knew his brain was all over the place, and he needed to focus. Taking Howard's hand, he drew him deeper into the screened porch, allowing the door to swing shut. "Please, sit. I have much to explain."

Nodding, Howard did as instructed and settled on the porch swing.

Zylen eased down beside him. Absently, still drawing his thoughts together, he began moving them.

"You're starting to freak me out a little," Howard murmured, squeezing his hand. "Talk to me."

Staring at where he held Howard's hand, Zylen began rubbing over the back, hoping to soothe him. "I don't mean to freak you out." He met Howard's gaze and smiled. The man was truly stunning. "It's just, I've never been in this situation before."

"What situation?" Howard turned partly toward him, bumping Zylen's leg with his knee. "A relationship? That *is* what we're headed for, right?"

"Yes, that, too, but no." Zylen grimaced. "I am not making any sense, am I?"

Howard chuckled softly. "Not too much. No."

"Okay, I will back up." Zylen blinked twice, cleared his throat, then focused on Howard. "I told you that you are my *stella guida*, my guiding star. That I'll be here for you forever."

Nodding, Howard murmured, "Yeah, that's the gist I got from ya."

"I'm being literal in that sense. You *chose* me, so after I spill in you, our bond will be complete. I'll never be able to leave

65

you, and my entire focus will be to create a safe, blissful environment around us, geared toward your happiness."

"Uh, no one can guarantee a safe, blissful environment," Howard replied with a smile. "We can only do the best we can to keep each other happy. We communicate and compromise and consider how our actions will impact our partner."

Zylen nodded slowly. "There's a bit more to it than that for us because—" He hesitated, feeling as if he was about to step off a cliff without knowing what was beneath him.

"Because?" Howard pressed, his voice low.

The crooning quality soothed Zylen, just as he'd probably intended.

Sighing, Zylen held his gaze as he took the plunge. "Because I'm not human, Howard. There are more on this planet that just humans. There always have been, but prejudices force them, force *us* to hide. Otherwise, our kind are hunted and killed . . . or worse."

Howard stared at him for a moment, and Zylen waited. Finally, his human asked, "Uh, can you explain that a little more, please?"

"Of course." Zylen hummed, tipping his head. "They are called paranormals, and humans have created many myths and legends about them, about us, too." He smiled, thinking of some of them. "Most of what is out there is utterly ridiculous."

"Name a type of paranormal."

Pleased that Howard was asking questions, Zylen told him, "The paranormals that reside in this realm are shifters. What you would call were-creatures, although they don't require the full moon to change, and they are completely cognizant while in animal form." Zylen watched Howard blink as his eyebrows ratcheted up. "Another would be vampires, but they are not allergic to garlic or holy water, and really, any being stabbed through the heart will die."

Zylen felt Howard's fingers curl in his, holding on very tightly, too tightly. He spotted the tension and saw the slight tremor. Wrapping his arm around Howard, Zylen pulled him tight against his side.

"I'm so sorry. I don't mean to freak you out. I told you I'd never explained this before, and I'm certain I'm completely botching it up."

Howard whispered, "Why are you claiming these things?" Lifting his head, he met his gaze. "Are you crazy? Are you on meds? Are you off your meds and you *should* be on them?" Pushing on his chest, Howard attempted to ease away from him. "Look, I understand mental illness can be tough, and I want to help, so please don't think I'm judging you, but—"

"I'll prove it if you sit still," Zylen whispered into his ear.

"Okay."

Zylen recognized the tone as placating. His *stella guida* didn't believe him. He'd known that could be a possibility.

"The saying *seeing is believing* came from somewhere, and this is a prime example," Zylen commented absently. Straightening a little, he lifted one hand to Howard's jaw as he rubbed the second up and down his back. "You have nothing to fear from me."

Then Zylen dropped his glamour.

Howard gasped and jerked in his hold.

Continuing to stare down at Howard, Zylen took in his response. He knew what the human could now see. His aura shown, making Zylen stunningly beautiful to the human eye. He flexed his wings, the feathers of various shades of brown filling the space between the swing and the wall. With the way Howard's gaze flicked to them, his lips parted in awe, Zylen couldn't help but smile. He didn't even have enough room to stretch them out fully.

"What—" Howard's voice cracked, and he swallowed twice before he could try again. "What are you?"

"I'm an angel, Howard." Zylen eased off the bench, carefully maneuvering his wings around the swing's chains. "And you, Howard." He knelt in front of Howard, urging him to spread his legs so he could slot between them. "You are the piece of my soul I didn't realize I was missing." Resting his arms along Howard's thighs, Zylen placed his hands on his hips. "I am so very grateful to have found you, my guiding star."

Howard sat gaping at him for what felt like an eternity before his eyes rolled to the back of his head, and he sagged against Zylen.

Sighing, Zylen cradled Howard to his chest. "Well, I suppose it could have gone worse," he muttered to himself.

"That's true."

Zylen clutched Howard to his chest as he spun to see the speaker. On instinct, he pulled his magick around him. Not a moment too soon, either, for a dart stabbed into his back. The second one bounced off his shield.

Growling softly, Zylen swept his gaze over the three men as he plucked the dart from his lower back. All wore dark shades and sported the same get-up as the three who'd attacked him the last time. He didn't know if they *were* the same ones, however.

"Hmmm, let's try that again," the middle man stated, firing another dart. Once again, it hit his shield. Lifting his hand to some kind of radio attached to his shoulder, he stated, "We're gonna need the coven on this one. He has some kind of shield up."

Zylen chuckled softly, even as he felt a wave of lethargy hit him. The dart must have been more potent than the last ones. Still, even being slightly compromised, he knew there was no way a circle of witches could overpower him.

"You should really leave now if you value your lives," Zylen warned while putting in a mental call to Lucha and

Wisner. "My friends aren't nearly as understanding of your attacks."

The speaker scoffed derisively. "What friends? Angels are solitary, aloof, and think they're better than everyone else. Angels don't have friends." He snickered as he tipped his chin toward them. "Until you find your guiding star and turn them into a sex slave."

"That is *not* the bond an angel has with our human," Zylen declared, righteous anger surging through him. "How dare you try to sully something so beautiful and pure."

Sneering, the speaker roared, "Humans aren't your playthings!"

"Aww, sure they are." Lucha eased from the shadows of the house on the left.

"I like playing with humans," Wisner taunted from the right. "I don't know. Three against two. Hardly seems fair."

"What the fuck, boss?" the guy on the left whispered. "Are those demons?"

"I thought demons were black," the man on the right muttered. "Could be gargoyles, though."

"Take 'em down," the middle man ordered, raising his weapon.

All three men fired darts at Lucha and Wisner. The pair didn't even bother to move. They just stood there and muttered a few words in the language of demons that Zylen didn't know. The darts missed them.

"Fuck!" the guy on the right swore. "Where are the witches?"

Lucha chuckled softly. "That's not a good idea."

"We think so," the man in the middle responded belligerently. "We're gonna take you all in. After we force the angel to bond with his human, we're gonna have an angel doing the hunters' bidding. We'll be heroes."

I can't wait for the praise Dorsey will heap on me. The hunter's excited thoughts came through loud and clear. *I'll be raised to his number one for sure this time.*

Hmm, Dorsey. I wonder if that's his first name or his last name. Either way, I have information to pass on to the paranormals searching for these guys.

Shaking his head, Wisner glanced between Zylen and Lucha. "Is this guy for real?" He thrust a thumb in the hunter's direction.

"I'm afraid he does seem to think so," Zylen stated, sending a mental message to the demons about keeping the humans talking. He wanted more information. Shifting Howard in his arms, he rose, then settled on the swing. He gently rocked his *stella guida* as he curled his wings around his human. "It's not surprising, since a human wouldn't think there could be rules about using the minions of one realm against the others."

Zylen smiled at the surprised expression on the humans' faces as they glanced between each other. The ones on the outside took a step backward, notably wary. The guy in the middle stood his ground, obviously having no self-preservation.

"Wh-What do you mean by realms?" the man on the left asked.

"Just how it sounds, dumbass," Lucha ridiculed. "Me and my friends ain't from around here."

Holy shit! There are whole other worlds out there? If we could find a way in . . . enslave them . . . oh, Dorsey is gonna have a field day with this.

Fighting back his urge to roll his eyes, Zylen shook his head. "We don't fight against each. We police our own kind."

"You got rogues," the man on the right countered. "They kill plenty of humans."

"Are you sayin' your serial killers don't do the exact same thing?" Wisner countered. "Every species has their evil trouble makers."

The pair on either side of the egomaniac actually glanced

at each other. If we continued talking, we might have even managed to get through to them.

Too bad the witches arrived.

CHAPTER TEN

Howard sniffed as he shifted restlessly on the lumpy as hell mattress. Something was burning. Tensing, fear for his house flooded him.

Except, he realized there was no way he was in his bed.

"Easy, Howard." Zylen's deep croon sounded in his ear. "You're safe in my arms. No harm will come to you."

At first, Howard relaxed. However, then the realization of who — or *what* — was holding him hit him.

Zylen wasn't human.

Jerking forward, Howard flailed. He slammed one hand into a hard chest and the other into something so soft and downy. It made him pause and look around.

Wings. I'm being cradled by wings. Holy fuck!

"Howard," Zylen purred, rubbing his palm over his scalp so he could cradle his nape. He lingered there, massaging lightly. "Look at me, handsome."

Taking a slow deep breath, Howard peered up and met Zylen's aqua gaze. The color seemed more intense than usual, but then that made sense. Zylen had been hiding part of himself.

"Zylen?"

"Welcome back, Howard."

Zylen dipped his head and pressed a soft, lingering kiss to his lips. Except, when Howard opened and the other man didn't deepen the kiss — instead breaking away — he frowned. Zylen smiled.

"As much as I want to ravage you, now really isn't the time

or place." Zylen lifted his gaze as he lowered his wings a little, creating a break in the feathers. "You remember those prejudice people we hide from? Well" — he sighed — "they found me. They want to kidnap you and use you against me."

Howard peered around his backyard and gaped. "Holy shit!"

The activity looked like something out of the *Twilight Zone* . . . or maybe some science fiction flick. Smoke drifted through the air, hovering a few inches off the ground. Lightning flashed, sparking from the hands of several women. Guys with guns hid behind trees and shot at . . . creatures.

Staring at the creatures the gunmen and women were facing off against, Howard felt a shiver go down his spine. The pair were tall and toned with white skin. They had wings, but not like Zylen's — bat-like instead of similar to a bird's. Plus, they were doing some chanting of their own.

The creatures jumped and lunged, rolled and dove, as they maneuvered around the women and men. They shot bolts of green . . . energy, perhaps . . . at the women, and it crackled around them. Every once in a while, whatever invisible shield the women had up would fail, and she would flop over. The white creatures cackled and teased their enemies, obviously having a heyday.

"What the hell is going on?" Howard meant to scream the words, but they only came out a whisper. Peering up at Zylen, he asked, "Why aren't you helping them?"

"Who?" Zylen tipped his head to the side.

Howard straightened, pointing at the women and men. "Them. The guys trying to take out those monsters!" Hearing the sigh from Zylen, he snapped his gaze to the beautiful man. "You're an angel, right? One of the good guys? So you should help!"

Zylen's smile appeared sad. "But, Howard, my *stella guida*, the humans are *not* the good guys. The *demons* are."

Gasping, Howard attempted to scramble from his lap, but Zylen wasn't having it. He wrapped his arms around Howard and clutched him close to his chest. While nuzzling Howard's neck, he began to talk.

"Do you remember me talking about how we hide because those with prejudices would threaten our safety? Our lives? These people are with that group. They wish to capture us. To cage us. To experiment on us. To force us to do things against our will. There is so much I still need to explain, but, Howard, please believe me when I say that those humans mean us harm."

Howard heard the desperation in Zylen's voice, the conviction. Could he believe it, though? After all, not long ago, he'd thought humans were alone in the universe.

"Those demons are called Lucha and Wisner. They are taunting those humans but not killing them," Zylen continued with his explanation. "They'll be questioned, and their minds erased, so they don't remember that paranormals exist." Lifting his head, Zylen held his gaze. "Then they'll be released to live out the rest of their days."

Wanting to believe that so badly, Howard searched Zylen's gaze. He saw the honesty there. The angel believed his words.

"How can you be certain?"

Zylen smiled. "I'm an angel, Howard. I can tell if another being is lying to me."

"So who told you that they'd be released, and how can their minds be erased?" Howard trembled as a new fear ripped through him. "Will my mind be erased?"

I don't want to forget my time with Zylen.

"No, *stella guida*. You are my star, remember? The missing piece of my soul." Zylen pressed a kiss to his temple. "How can I care for you if you do not know me?"

Howard nodded. That made sense.

"And I was assured by these demons' master, Pestilence."

"Pestilence," Howard parroted. "Who's that?"

"A horseman of the apocalypse," Zylen claimed.

Tensing, Howard cried, "They're real, too?"

"Lots of things are real, human star," a soft tenor revealed, drawing Howard's attention to his left.

Taking in the pale man standing there, Howard gasped. He had long white-blond hair, slightly sallow features, and pale amber eyes. His frame was slightly hunched, and he carried a hunter's bow as well as a quiver of arrows.

"Congratulations, Zylen," the male continued. "I was happy to hear of your great fortune."

"Thank you, Horseman," Zylen replied with a bow of his head.

"Pestilence," the guy corrected.

Zylen chuckled. "Pestilence."

"You're a horseman of the apocalypse?" Howard asked, his shock not allowing him to censor his words.

"I am."

"Where's your horse?" *Yep, I'm gonna get smote.*

Pestilence laughed, the sound a little raspy. "Why do people always ask about our horses?"

"Perhaps because your pictures always have you on your mounts," Zylen offered. "And you are called Horsemen, after all."

"Hmm. Good point." Pestilence smiled at Howard. "My horse would not fit in your screened-in porch, Howard."

"You know my name." Howard snapped his gaze to Zylen. "How? That can't be good, can it?"

"The Four Horsemen of the Apocalypse are charged with keeping the balance between the planet you live on and the occupants of it." Pestilence's smile held an indulgent quality, as did his tone. "We know everyone who has ever existed."

"Damn," Howard muttered. "That's a lot of names."

"Indeed."

"How are you feeling now, my *stella guida*," Zylen asked.

He rubbed the backs of his fingers along his jaw. "Better?"

Howard nodded slowly, then took in his surroundings again. "Why are we just sitting here?"

"Well, my creator advised me to let the demons handle it," Zylen stated, and Howard realized he would have more questions on that later, but he remained focused on Zylen, since he kept talking. "And one of those men shot me with a rather potent dart in an attempt to kidnap us, so I'm feeling a bit of fatigue as my body fights off the effects."

Following where Zylen pointed, Howard spotted a feathered dart on the floor of his porch. "Those bastards."

Pestilence laughed.

After the horseman settled, the silence registered to Howard. He looked around and saw the two demons high-fiving each other. All the humans were sprawled on the ground.

"Casualties?" Pestilence asked as he exited the porch.

"No, Master," one of the males claimed with a bow. "They will all live."

"Good." Pestilence rested a hand on each of the demons' shoulders. "Did you have fun?"

"Yes, Master," the other male answered with a wide grin.

Pestilence smiled at his demon. "Your *amina* is near, Lucha." He released both and dipped his hand into his tunic. Then he held up a scroll. "I'll take it from here. Good hunting, my demon. You deserve it."

The expression that crossed the demon's face—Lucha—could only be called . . . elation.

"What's an *amina*?" Howard whispered, wondering what kind of hunting there would be.

"A demon's *amina* is similar to an angel's *stella guida*. After a thousand years of service, a demon is granted an *amina* to bond with and love."

Gaping, Howard asked, "Demons have souls?"

Zylen shook his head. "No. They share the soul of whoever

their *amina* is."

"Why would—"

Placing his fingertips over Howard's lips, Zylen smiled down at him. "I'll answer every question in good time. But what do you say we head inside? Pestilence will handle things here." A pained expression slid over his features. "I'm a bit fatigued from the constant magick use required to keep my protective shield in place around us, coupled with the drugs they hit me with. I would like to lie down and hold you if that's okay."

Howard nodded even as more questions popped into his head. "Yeah, yeah." He jumped to his feet as soon as Zylen lowered his wings and loosened his hold. Pivoting, he offered his hand, which Zylen took. As he helped the angel to his feet, Howard hated seeing the way the big strong male stumbled.

My god, the angel was attacked by hunters on my back porch. Shit, what a weird thing to think!

Zylen chuckled softly. "It'll get easier."

"Did I say that out loud?" Howard didn't think he had.

"Sorry, Howard." Zylen's cheeks pinked a little, betraying his embarrassment. "One of the abilities an angel wields is reading minds. If the person is exuberant enough or passionate enough about their thoughts, I can pick up on them."

"Well, that's . . . kinda rude, actually."

Indignation filled Howard even as he helped Zylen into the house. Then he glanced over his shoulder, spotting Pestilence and the other demon sending the bodies . . . somewhere.

God, more questions.

"Are we safe here?"

"We are," Zylen assured. "While you were out, Pestilence assured me that he placed wards around your home for several miles. No one with ill intent will be able to approach while I'm recovering."

"Okay." Howard started them up the stairs. "And the

mind-reading thing? That's how you've been able to antici-pate certain things with me, huh?"

Howard recalled asking Zylen how he knew what he was thinking.

"Yes," Zylen admitted. "After we bond, I'll teach you how to guard your thoughts." Rubbing up and down Howard's spine, he slipped his palm beneath Howard's shirt, sending a thrill along his flesh. "We'll also be able to speak to each other telepathically. I'll teach you that, too."

"Seriously?"

"Mmm-hmm."

Well, that's sorta cool.

Zylen chuckled, telling Howard he'd picked up on the thought.

An idea popped into Howard's head.

"Do you think you'll have the energy to do this?" Howard asked as he settled Zylen on the bed.

"Do what?"

Then Howard filled his thoughts with his desire. He pictured them both naked, his ass up and his head down. Zylen crouched behind him, pistoning his impressive girth in and out of his chute. The angel's wings were spread for balance as he hammered into him, driving them both closer and closer toward release.

Zylen growled Howard's name, but that was in real life.

In the next instant, both their clothes had disappeared. Howard didn't know how or where, but he didn't care.

His angel grabbed him and tossed him onto the comforter, face first. He sprawled over him, wedging his prodigious girth into his crack. As he slowly rutted, rubbing his leaking crown against Howard's soft skin, he whispered into his ear.

"Where's your lube, Howard?"

Oh, yeah. This mind thingy could be cool after all.

CHAPTER ELEVEN

Zylen's body flushed hot, fire coursing through his veins, burning away any hint of fatigue. The thoughts that had been coursing through Howard's brain hit him like a flash fire in a pan. He couldn't help but combust.

When Howard pointed to the nightstand on the right, Zylen stretched to reach it. He opened the drawer and peered inside. His heart thundered in his chest when he spotted the tube.

Grabbing it, Zylen popped the cap. He wanted to be patient, to show his *stella guida* how much he meant to him. With that thought in mind, he took a deep breath and tightened his grip on some sliver of control.

"Easy, my star," Zylen crooned before kissing over one of Howard's shoulders. He nibbled at the nape of his neck before starting down his spine. "I wish to please you. To show you how much I care."

Howard panted softly, shivering under his touch and pushing into his ministrations.

Zylen's erection ached and throbbed with each move Howard made. His forever love was so responsive, so perfect. He moaned Zylen's name between mewls of pleasure.

Working down Howard's broad back, Zylen licked and nipped along his powerful torso. He traced the flesh with his tongue, enjoying the salty masculine flavor of the man. His skin felt so soft and warm over the hard muscle beneath.

When Zylen reached the base of Howard's spine, he helped him up on his knees. His star immediately spread his knees wide. Zylen moaned upon seeing the way Howard opened for him.

"Perfect," Zylen muttered as he dipped his tongue into his crack, licking along the hidden flesh. Bliss fired through his veins, and his dick twitched when he heard Howard whimper and arch, pushing toward his tongue. "So responsive. Love."

"Z-Zylen. Zylen, please," Howard whined.

"Gotta open you up," Zylen warned, pouring lube onto his fingers. "Don't wanna hurt you."

When Zylen had been waiting for Howard to get home—in between bouts of panic about how to explain paranormals—he'd searched for gay sex instructions on his phone. The results had been . . . enlightening. He wondered how many different things Howard would be up to trying.

A talk for another day.

Zylen pressed his slicked digit against Howard's striated opening, massaging the muscle lightly at first, then harder. When it fluttered beneath his touch, he pushed. Hot muscle encased his digit, seeming to suck it in swiftly.

Sucking in a harsh breath, Zylen reached down and gripped the base of his shaft. He moaned as he continued to work his finger in and out, unable to believe how tight Howard was. Zylen didn't know how he was going to fit.

"Hurry, Zy," Howard pleaded. "Another finger. I can take it. I've fingered myself. I've used toys. Do it."

The image of Howard sliding his digits in and out of his own ass popped into his mind. He whimpered, knowing he would love to see that someday.

Obeying his *stella guida*, Zylen pressed in a second finger. With the way his erection throbbed and drooled, he knew he needed to hurry. His dick felt so hard it could snap off at any second . . . or his orgasm would no longer be denied.

Neither option would be good.

Zylen added a third finger, pegging Howard's gland and reveling in his human's bliss-infused cries.

"Now, now, now." Howard's chanting finally registered to Zylen's foggy brain.

"You sure?" Zylen had to ask. His erection had quite a bit more girth than three fingers.

Howard growled as he scowled over his shoulder. "You don't and I'm gonna flip you and ride you anyway."

As hot as that sounded, even pulling a spurt of pre-cum from Zylen's dick, he wanted to fulfill his human's other fantasy instead.

Zylen pulled his fingers free. He grabbed the lube and added some directly to his shaft. At the feel of the cool liquid, he hissed. Wrapping his wet fingers around himself, Zylen quickly smoothed it over his flesh.

Knee-walking forward, Zylen levered over Howard. He gripped one meaty cheek in his clean palm and pulled it sideways. Then he used his other hand to guide his uncut crown to Howard's stretched hole.

"Yesssss," Howard hissed, obviously feeling him there. "Do it. Please, do it."

As much as the begging sent spikes of adrenaline through Zylen's body, he needed to give Howard what he desired even more. Zylen pushed forward, then harder. Finally, he watched his crown pop past the tight ring of muscles.

Hearing Howard's bark of surprise, the noise filled with pain, yanked a whine of dismay from Zylen's throat. "I'm sorry," he cried, starting to pull back even though it was the hardest thing he had ever experienced. "So sorry."

"No!" Howard reached back and grabbed his thigh, stilling his movement. "Just stop. Give me a sec. That was" — he huffed a few breaths — "a lot."

Resting his weight on his left hand, Zylen gripped Howard's hip with his right. He pressed his forehead against his human's nape and struggled to take in deep gulps of air. Then he recalled a bit of advice he'd read.

Zylen slid his right hand under Howard, feeling for his dick. Finding it semi-hard, he began to tug in long smooth strokes—root to tip, root to tip. He started mouthing kisses along his shoulder blade as he did his best to keep still.

To Zylen's relief—and pleasure—Howard's dick quickly began to refill. His lover sighed and tipped his head, offering him more room to kiss and nuzzle. Zylen felt his teeth tingle in an unfamiliar way, and the urge to bite hit him.

Knowing it was natural, Zylen accepted it. He would wait, however, wanting to offer his lover as much pleasure as his inexperience would allow.

We have eternity to learn each other. I can't wait.

Finally, Howard's clench on his crown eased.

Zylen still waited, fondling Howard's erection, adding in a caress over his ball sack with each stroke.

"Move, Zy," Howard whispered.

That time, Zylen didn't question him. He moved . . . ever-so-slowly. Sinking his dick in a little more, then retreating, repeating the process over and over until his hefty shaft speared his lover as deeply as he could go.

Once Zylen had finally bottomed out, he groaned low in his throat. Never would he have guessed at the feel of being buried so intimately within another. He never wanted to leave.

That, however, was unrealistic.

Zylen had only managed to keep still for a few heartbeats when the driving, burning instinct to rut chased away all semblance of control.

Growling around the flesh Zylen worked with his mouth, he pulled out only to snap his hips forward again. He roared as exquisite sensations shot through his dick and warmed his groin. His testicles tingled and tightened. Zylen had to do it over and over and over, plundering Howard's body.

"Zylen," Howard shouted his name. His body jolted, arching, meeting him thrust for thrust. "Yes!"

Relishing Howard's cry, Zylen reared onto his knees. He wrapped his left arm around his human's torso and hauled him up, pressing his chest to his back. Continuing his onslaught on Howard's hole, Zylen used the momentum of his snapping hips to drive his *stella guida*'s erection through his grip. Spreading his wings for balance, he sped up his thrusts, his mind consumed with spilling and marking his lover.

Howard lifted his arms and wrapped them around Zylen's neck, holding Zylen's face to his neck. He felt his teeth lengthen even as his balls lifted even higher. His orgasm was there, so close.

"Come, Howard." Zylen snarled the order, his voice deeper and rougher than he'd ever heard it. "Do it now. Feel me claim you."

Screaming Zylen's name, Howard obeyed. His erection pulsed in his hand, and his chute rippled along Zylen's length. The dick Zylen held belched burst after burst of creamy seed.

"Mine!"

Zylen couldn't hold in the primal cry as he seated his erection as deep in Howard as he could go and poured his release into him. Moaning, he froze, his dick throbbing and twitching. He felt as if he shot forever, and spots danced across his vision.

The pain in his gums registered, telling him his claiming fangs had descended. Resting back on his calves, keeping Howard as close as two bodies could be, he sank his canines into his *stella guida*'s flesh. As the blood welled around his teeth and he drank Howard's life-giving fluid, he heard his human's gasp of surprise.

To Zylen's relief, in the next instant, Howard moaned and shuddered in his hold. He twitched as his body tumbled through another orgasm. Hearing him moan his name, Zylen smiled as he drank another mouthful of his blood.

With Howard resting all his weight on him, his chest heaving, and whimpering moans escaping him as he twitched with aftershocks, Zylen didn't think he'd ever seen anything more beautiful.

Finally sated, Zylen eased his teeth free of Howard's shoulder. He swallowed once more before lapping over the tooth marks, sealing them, and locking his saliva inside. The change would begin, not that it would be noticeable on the outside.

"Wh-What was that?" Howard slurred, sounding almost as drunk as he'd been the previous evening.

Zylen grinned, pleased with himself. "That, my guiding star, was me claiming you." Carefully, he eased them to their sides, keeping his still hard erection buried in Howard's channel. He began moving slowly, in and out, loving the feel of it there. "My saliva is what keeps extending your life to match mine."

"Really?" Howard sounded a bit more alert. "Extended? By like . . . how much?"

Freezing, Zylen realized he should have explained this first. "Um, eternity?"

Howard barked a laugh, but when Zylen didn't join in, he turned his head and met his gaze. "Really?"

Zylen nodded. "Yes."

Pain filled Howard's expressive hazel eyes. "But my family," he whispered.

"I can heal your sister's barren state, so you can always have family with you, after a fashion," Zylen offered. "Nieces, nephews, great-nieces and nephews." Sighing, he pressed a kiss to Howard's neck. "I'm sorry. That is the way of paranormals, my star. We outlive humans."

Howard sighed deeply before peering back at him again. "I know my sister and her husband would love that. Thank you."

"Then I shall," Zylen vowed.

"Wait." Howard reached back and slid his fingers through Zylen's hair. "I thought you all weren't supposed to tell humans unless they're your other half."

"Due to the aggressiveness of the hunters in this area, your family will need to be warned. Protection will be provided." Teasing at Howard's neck, Zylen admitted, "These are dangerous times, my star. I'm sorry."

"Not your fault," Howard countered. Then he clenched his channel and groaned. "Holy shit. We're talking about family and hunters, and you're still hard inside me. How is that possible?"

Zylen grinned as he started moving again. It drew a deep moan from Howard. Reaching down, he discovered his human was growing hard, too.

"I'll need to anoint your insides with my seed several times this evening before I soften," Zylen explained, kissing and nibbling at his nape. "Don't worry. You'll enjoy it each time."

Howard snickered. *Anointed.*

Zylen heard Howard repeat the word to himself.

"Making fun of me?" Zylen asked, teasing. He didn't mind. After all, he was old. "Naughty lover."

Zylen reached up and pinched a nipple.

Sucking in a harsh gasp, Howard trembled in his hold.

"Oh, interesting." Zylen squeezed Howard's bud again, lighter that time, then harder. The move drew a moan from his lover. "So much to learn about you," he rumbled into Howard's ear. "I can't wait to get started."

Panting harshly, Howard gripped Zylen's forearm with one hand and his hip with the other. "Th-Then anoint away."

Zylen chuckled huskily as he began to pleasure Howard anew. "Don't mind if I do."

So he did.

CHAPTER TWELVE

"Goddamnit, I still can't believe I couldn't talk my way out of this," Howard grumbled, his face heating as he felt Zylen's thick yet nimble fingers doing his bowtie. If he'd known the affair was black tie when he'd first heard about the auction, he would have flat out told them no.

Instead, everything that night had ended up about him coming out.

Howard and Zylen had been living in his home for the last two weeks together. He'd introduced his partner to his mother, who'd asked a million questions, including some embarrassing ones. When she'd learned that they hadn't known each other very long, she'd asked, "Could maybe you be confused . . . about the whole gay thing?"

Never in Howard's life had he laughed so hard.

She didn't ask that question again, although she still had a troubled expression from time to time. In truth, however, Howard thought that might be from the angel and paranormal revelation. She met several men—demons—who used a glamour to disguise themselves.

They were introduced as paranormal security. They were the Horseman of War's men—big, heavily built, and sort of scary-looking. Still, Zylen had assured him that they were just what his family needed until the threat from the hunters had passed.

When Zylen had offered to correct the issue of Lilibeth being barren, she'd cried.

Understandable.

Zylen had rubbed his palm over her belly, just a touch really, and said it was done.

Lilibeth had appeared hopeful, Macon wary. Due to the word of an angel, they were going to try again.

"Your sister is pregnant," Zylen whispered to me, smiling. "Three days. We'll visit them often so I can monitor her until she's far enough along. Then you can encourage her to test."

Barking a laugh, Howard threw his arms over Zylen's shoulders. He hugged his angel as tight as he could. Lilibeth's inability had hung over all of them for so long that it felt like such a burden had been lifted.

Howard even felt tears sting the backs of his eyes.

"Hey, I didn't tell you to make you cry, my *stella guida*," Zylen rumbled, gripping Howard's face in his big hands. Carefully, he rubbed his thumbs under his eyes, wiping away a couple of tears that had actually escaped. Waggling his brows, Zylen told him, "I just wanted to give you something to think about other than this auction."

Just that quickly, Howard groaned.

Laughing, Zylen gripped his hand and led him out of the house. "You know I'm going to be the one buying you, so what are you worried about?"

"I still don't get how you plan to do that. You're an angel. You have no income."

Zylen barked a laugh as he locked the front door behind us. Pointing at his *Jeep*, he ordered, "Watch."

Howard felt the hairs on his arms lift on end as Zylen whispered something under his breath. Between one breath and the next, the *Jeep* changed. Instead of the older green vehicle, there was a massive pile of cash. Not just cash, either, but gems and jewelry and gold and silver dishes and shit.

"Holy crapballs," Howard whispered. He'd been trying to clean up his language, even though Zylen assured him that it didn't bother him. In turn, Howard had explained that realizing how often he cussed that it had begun to bother him. It was a work in progress. "How's that possible?"

Except, as Howard started toward the huge pile, Zylen tightened his grip where their fingers were threaded. With another few words, the pile of goodies returned to the form of a *Jeep.*

"Hey!"

Zylen just laughed, then led the way to Howard's truck. "Come on, my star."

Once they were both buckled in and were on their way — Howard driving and Zylen comfortable in the passenger seat — Howard asked again, "So, I understand that it's magick, but what? Do you just create stuff out of thin air?"

"No, my love. No one can make something from thin air. Not even the creator."

Howard nodded slowly. They'd had a few talks about the creator, and he sort of equated him to what some people would call God. He was an ancient, powerful being that lived in another dimension. His angels policed humans in a small way, encouraging them to be kinder, nicer, and more loving to others.

Oddly enough, the demons were created by the gods known as Olympians.

He found it all weird and confusing, but he was trying.

"So, where does it come from?" Howard pressed.

"It's a transformation spell," Zylen explained. "I take something of equal matter and turn it into something else. That's why I couldn't allow you to take even one gem." When Howard cast a questioning look Zylen's way, he told him, "If I didn't want a part on the *Jeep* missing, I'd have to use a patch of grass or a tree root or something else to complete it. It was just easier not to mess with matter dynamics."

"Oh, gotcha." As a plumber who always had to make certain everything fit just right, Howard understood. "So, regardless of how much I cost, you'll just come up with that much cash, huh?"

"Already did," Zylen told him with a wink. "I turned a number of rocks in your garden into gems last week. I used your stationery to create provenance records. We have a joint account with a couple of million in it."

Howard nearly drove off the road. "What!"

Zylen just chuckled as he reached over and squeezed his thigh.

Just that fast, Howard found himself distracted. His dick twitched, and his groin warmed. He shifted restlessly in his seat, his chute clenching with need.

"Behave," Zylen growled, tightening his hold and stilling Howard's movements. "I'll take care of all that after the auction."

The auction. Right. Definite boner killer.

Zylen laughed again, telling Howard that he'd picked up on his thoughts.

Yep. Another work in progress.

Still, Howard found it cool to be able to chat with Zylen while at work, all in his head.

One day Howard had asked, "What are you up to today?"

After all, what did an angel do all day while his partner was working?

"I'm within a block of you," Zylen had admitted. "I'm searching people's minds for ill intent toward, well, anyone. I'm spreading happiness, love, and acceptance."

"Huh. Like a modern day cupid."

Zylen had laughed in his mind. "Not that kind of love, my star."

Howard always smiled when Zylen called him that. He felt the man's love through their bond. It was a heady sensation, being loved by an angel.

They arrived at the banquet, and Howard snickered under his breath at the look of distaste on the valet's face when he had to drive his truck. Yes, his vehicle was dinged up and older, but she still ran great. Howard came from money, but he was never one to put on airs.

Handing the keys to the valet, Howard still tipped the man generously before straightening his tuxedo. Then he headed around the vehicle and smiled at Zylen. The angel offered his hand, which Howard took.

Out of the corner of his eye, Howard noticed several disappointed-looking women.

That's right, ladies. He's all mine.

Zylen dipped his head and whispered, "Yes, I am."

Howard grinned.

Heading into the huge hotel, Howard quickly located the massive room used to host the gala. There were crystal chandeliers overhead, marble floors beneath their feet, and silver flatware on the tables. Waiters and waitresses in uniform carried trays of complimentary champagne and finger foods.

A woman immediately offered them champagne.

Howard took one.

To his surprise, Zylen did as well.

After taking a sip, Howard mind-spoke to him. *I thought you didn't drink.*

Zylen's warm chuckle pushed through his mind as the corners of his lips curved up a little. *I said I don't get drunk.* Perhaps Zylen felt Howard's confusion, for he added something more. *Human beverages do very little due to my genetics. I'd probably have to drink several bottles of straight eighty-proof to even start to feel it.*

You up for that? Howard couldn't help but tease his man.

"No," Zylen answered out loud, his expression changing to something a little haunted. Pulling Howard out of the stream of traffic, Zylen tipped his head down and met his gaze. "Pestilence told me I was unconscious for six days before they rescued me. Another two after that, and weak as a kitten for a couple more. *Never* will I risk compromising my senses." Untangling their fingers, Zylen cradled Howard's cheek. "Your safety is far too important for something so foolish as that, my *stella guida*."

Howard's throat tightened up, and he had to take a deep breath. Letting it out slowly, he whispered, "I'm sorry that happened to you, and I feel the same about you." He began to set aside the champagne.

Zylen gave a quick shake of his head as he smiled. "Don't do that." Dipping further, he pecked a kiss to Howard's lips. Then he grinned at him. "I happen to know that my strapping, handsome plumber would have to drink several bottles of champagne in swift succession to begin to feel it."

Grinning and relaxing, Howard arched one brow. "Oh, really?"

Laughing, Zylen wrapped his arm around Howard's waist and started them moving again. "I do. Especially since you told me exactly how much whiskey you had that first night I stayed over."

Howard groaned at the memory.

So embarrassing.

He hadn't actually expected Zylen to stay, since he hadn't understood his angel's nature at the time.

Still, Howard was glad he had, embarrassment and all. He was even more grateful for the fact that his angel had given him a partial healing the next morning. It had certainly explained how rapidly his hangover had diminished.

"Ugh, god, that is so disgusting," a loud feminine voice called belligerently. "I can't believe they let you in here amongst us decent folk."

Even recognizing the voice, Howard still had to bite back a groan when he spotted Shirley. She would have looked beautiful in her pale lavender sheath dress that set off her blonde hair and blue eyes in a lovely manner. Unfortunately, with her flushed cheeks, angry scowl, and hate-filled eyes—yeah, not so much.

There were several soft gasps as others turned to watch the drama unfold.

Shirley stalked forward, and that was when Howard noticed the slight unsteadiness to her gait. Perhaps the red flush to her cheeks wasn't all due to outrage. Lifting her white-glove-covered hand, she pointed at him.

"You are an abomination and a disgrace," Shirley declared, looking up at Howard. With her stilettos, she was only about an inch or so shorter than him. She opened her mouth and turned to spew what was probably more vitriol at Zylen, but perhaps she realized just how big he was, for she turned back to Howard. "Disgracing your sweet mother that way. No one is going to bid on you. I'll make sure of it."

Not too long ago, Howard would have been absolutely mortified to be on the receiving end of Shirley's outburst. Now, however, he felt . . . well, pity . . . for her. She was making a spectacle of herself, and no one was paying any mind to him.

"Shirley, hey, come on." A handsome, auburn-haired man with black-framed glasses wrapped his arm around her waist. "Let it go." He glanced Howard's way, an apology written all over his face. "Come have some of these delicious salmon crostini's."

"Absolutely not," Shirley shrieked. "Do you know what they are?" She pointed at us dramatically. "They're faggots. Homos. Sodomites." Her voice grew louder, shriller, with every slur. "Abominations! They need to leave!"

"I'm sorry, Miss, but it's you who will have to leave." A big man in a smart suit gripped her arm. "This establishment doesn't tolerate any kind of harassment here."

She screamed bloody murder.

Her date released her, looking shocked as she bucked in the big man's hold.

Huh. Look at that. This place has bouncers.

As the big guy led Shirley from the room, her date took a couple of steps after her. Then he paused, clearly torn. "I-I'm really sorry." He turned again to follow her.

"Hey," Howard found himself calling. "The bouncer didn't say anything about *you* needing to leave."

The man's face flushed an even deeper shade of red, and he glanced around uncertainly.

Howard stuck out his hand. "I'm Howard Burnside. This is my partner, Zylen." He used his head to indicate his angel. "Don't let Shirley's dramatics ruin your evening."

"R-Robert Thinter," he replied uncertainly. "Uh, Bob." His brows furrowed, almost hidden beneath his glasses. "You know Shirley?"

As Howard shook and released Bob's hand, he nodded. "I do. Shirley's older sister is married to my sister's husband's best friend."

Bob's mouth gaped.

Howard laughed. "Well, that was a lot to take in. Sorry."

"Uh—"

Hearing his mother call, Howard turned and grinned at her. "Hey, Ma. You look amazing."

She did, too. Her blonde hair was swept in an elegant up-do. She had on the pearls her father had bought her for their tenth wedding anniversary. The flowing pale green dress accentuated the green in her hazel eyes, and she appeared flushed with happiness.

"I found us a table. Come on. Dinner will start in a minute, and they'll fill up fast."

Howard turned to a still clearly confused and shell-shocked Bob. "You want to join us? Is there room, Ma?"

His mother beamed at him even as she took Zylen's arm and used him to escort her through the throng. "Any friend of Howard's is a friend of mine. Come on."

After winking at Zylen, Howard gripped Bob's upper arm. "Come on, man. Let's go sit. I'll set ya up with a drink."

"Okay."

As Howard followed his mother and his partner across the room, escorting someone who might turn out to be a new friend, he couldn't help but feel content. He had an amazing partner, a loving family, a fulfilling job with friends, and a bright future ahead. Sure, there might be bumps along the way with the hunters, but he knew his new paranormal friends could handle it.

Howard settled at the table next to Zylen. Resting his hand on his angel's thigh, he squeezed.

In response, Zylen leaned over and kissed him.

Yep. Life is dang near perfect.

Plus, as promised, Zylen outbid everyone at the auction, earning them an amazing date.

Interestingly enough, it was Leland Cross who brought in the most money.

As Howard danced with Zylen, his memory flitted to a couple of weeks before, and he couldn't help but think at his angel, *Maybe there's a certain blond-haired demon in his future.*

Zylen chuckled softly.

Maybe we should introduce them.

Snickering, Howard nodded.

Maybe.

The world could never have enough love in it.

YOU MAY ALSO ENJOY THE FOLLOWING FROM EXTASY BOOKS INC:

Don't Badger Me
Charlie Richards

Excerpt

Deacon read a second garage listing and hoped it wasn't run by a homophobe, too. After making a mental note of the directions, he lifted it off the kickstand and began wheeling it down the street. At least with his shifter strength, pushing the motorcycle was easy.

As soon as Deacon had heard that his brother Daevon had chosen to resign as a college professor and approach a nomadic alpha to join his pack—or gang, as they called it—Deacon had decided he would do the same. He hadn't had the opportunity to spend much time with his brother in over forty years. As a shifter, a paranormal living in a human world, he had to remake his identity every few decades.

The last time around, Deacon had headed to Chicago to be a firefighter, while Daevon had found a position in another city. Neither of them had had much free time. For the first time in a long time, Deacon had appreciated the changes in technology, but talking over a computer wasn't the same as frolicking together in animal form.

Thinking about his brother, Deacon realized he would need to call the man and let him know he wasn't going to make the rendezvous.

"As soon as I have something to tell him," Deacon muttered as the sign for the second garage came into view. The place appeared old and dingy, but at least, there was a glowing open in the window.

Deacon left his Triumph in the parking lot and headed into the office. Seeing no one behind the counter of the dirty room, he grimaced. He could hear clanging and talking coming from an open door to the left of the counter, so he knew someone was there.

"Hurry up with that oil change, Axel," a man ordered. "You were supposed to have that done this morning."

"Yes, sir," a deep voice responded softly.

Deacon knew that only his shifter hearing allowed him to make it out. The bass tones caused a warm flutter in his gut, and he almost hummed appreciatively. Having already been singled out for being gay stayed his reaction.

Instead, Deacon headed for the door and hollered, "Hello, the garage?"

"Yeah!" responded the first voice from deep in the bay behind an older Dodge pick-up.

Stopping in the doorway, Deacon swept his gaze over the area. He spotted movement in the back and waited. As he watched an overweight man in filthy coveralls lumbering toward him, he tried to breathe shallowly.

The scent of grease, oil, and other vehicle fluids hung heavy in the air. To his surprise, however, there was something else, too. He took a slow, deeper inhale, and heat and need began pooling in his gut.

Oh, damn! Do I seriously smell my mate in here?

With the way the heavyset man stared at him with narrowed eyes and a curled lip, Deacon prayed to whatever gods cared to listen that it wasn't him. Great. Another homophobe. Doing his best to ignore it, Deacon dipped his chin in a nod of greeting.

"Hello, sir," Deacon greeted. "I think the stator went out on my motorcycle. Can you take a look?"

The man looked Deacon up and down, his expression easy to read. "Axel, take care of this customer." Then he turned and walked away.

Oooookay. At least he's not my mate. His nasty BO just about knocked me outta my boots!

Which leaves Axel.

Deacon shoved his hands into his pockets as he spotted another form separate from the shadows in the back. The guy's shoulders were wide but a little hunched. He limped on his right leg, his steps uneven. With his face turned a little, his shaggy hair hid most of the features on his right side.

"This way, please, sir," the man—Axel, evidently—indicated the front room.

Taking a step backward, Deacon pivoted and allowed the man to pass him. At the same time, he took a discreet sniff. The human's odor was mixed with oil and grease, but underneath that, it was all masculine and all delicious.

Mmmm . . . oh, that's so good.

Deacon followed close behind Axel, enjoying the view of his ass, even in his coveralls. Watching him move, he wondered what caused the limp. Then Axel turned and rounded the counter, and Deacon spotted the scars up the right side of his neck, disappearing beneath his shaggy auburn hair.

Axel reached under the counter and pulled out a piece of paper, placing it before him. "Please fill out this form, sir," he murmured, lifting his left hand and pushing his hair behind his ear. Axel glanced up to look at him, revealing wary blue eyes. His focus slipped over Deacon's shoulder and out the front window. Then he met Deacon's gaze again. "You think it's the stator, sir?"

"Please, call me Deacon," Deacon offered, sliding the form close and picking up the pen on the counter. "And, yeah. All the signs are there. Dimming headlights, decreased power, and finally, the fuel pump shut off." As Deacon filled out the form, he took advantage of the moment to cast quick glances at the man. "The guy I bought it from said he thought it might be going out. It's that time." Shrugging, Deacon cast a wry smile Axel's way. "I was hoping to make it to where I was going before it happened, but oh well."

Deacon realized his mate was bigger and broader than him. His body appeared fit, although the baggy clothing made it tough to tell how muscled he was. While Deacon stood five-foot-eleven, he knew his mate had to be a couple of inches more, since he stood just a smidge taller than him even though he was hunched.

Axel lowered his focus to the paper. "I'm sorry, sir," he rumbled, tapping the form with his left hand. "I either need an address, or I'll need to ask you to pre-pay. Capson's rules."

It didn't miss Deacon's attention how Axel hadn't called him by his name. He also figured Capson was his dick boss.

Needing to figure out a way to connect with Axel, Deacon stared down at the form. He didn't have an address, right then. While he could easily pre-pay, an idea formed. Having already experienced prejudice from a couple of people, Deacon didn't want to make Axel a target while he got to know the man.

Which means I have to be discreet.

"I don't have an address, Axel," Deacon stated, resting his hand on the counter close to his mate's. "How about I pay your shop for a stator for my bike? Can we do that?"

Axel lifted his chin a little and met his gaze. The hair still fell across his face, but it was enough to reveal why the man hid. The scarring extended up his neck and across his cheek.

Ah, that's why he hides. Bet scarring is causing his limp, too. Just how bad is it?

Deacon kept the sadness for Axel's struggle off his face. Seeing as his mate obviously hid, he didn't want to draw attention to it. Instead, he arched one brow, silently entreating him to answer the question.

"I can't do that, sir," Axel murmured, shaking his head. "But there's an auto parts store three miles away, east of town." Lowering his gaze, he added, "They'll probably have it in stock, but if not, they can order it."

Nodding, Deacon was pleased Axel would at least talk to him and share information. It was more than what the other pair of men had done. He wondered if it was the mate-pull at work.

"Thank you, Axel," Deacon replied quietly. "I—"

"Axel!" Capson called from the other room. "Where you at, boy?"

When Axel rolled his eyes, Deacon smirked. "See you around," he rumbled, dipping his head.

After spotting Axel's answering nod, Deacon turned and headed out of the office. As the door swung closed behind him, he heard Axel reply, "Sorry, sir. He refused to pre-pay or give an address."

Deacon placed his helmet on his head and pulled out his phone. After connecting it to his headgear's Bluetooth function, he dialed his brother. While waiting for Daevon to answer, he began wheeling his motorcycle down the road. Deacon recalled seeing a sign for a government-run campground ten miles before the town. At least they wouldn't be able to refuse him.

Guess I'll get to use the tent in my saddlebag.

"Hey, little brother," Daevon greeted. "You still on track to make it?"

"Afraid not," Deacon replied as he walked. He kept an eye on the traffic, since he didn't want to get run over by a homophobe. "My bike broke down. I'm in a small town called Rusty Cave in Wisconsin."

"Broke your bike already?" Daevon sounded surprised. "You bought that older model you were telling me about, didn't you? The Triumph. Told you not to."

"I think it was Fate that caused my infatuation, actually," Deacon replied. Then he grinned. "I just found my mate."

Daevon laughed. "That's fantastic! Congrats, little bro. Is he gonna come with you? How long until your bike is fixed?"

"This town is full of homophobes, so I'm going to try to convince him to move on with me. Time will tell, though." Deacon heard the roar of an engine and glanced over his shoulder. "Jee-zus!"

Deacon jumped backward, yanking his bike with him. It was a good thing he had paranormal strength, or he wouldn't have been able to move it enough. The big black pick-up would have sideswiped him.

"Fucking homophobic bastards in this town," Deacon snarled. "Some asshat just tried to mow me down with his truck."

Growling softly, Daevon ordered, "Be careful until we get there."

"We?" Deacon asked as he continued walking.

Daevon hummed. "Alpha Kontra is near enough to over-hear our conversation. He doesn't like bullies and thinks the good people of the town need a re-education."

Deacon couldn't help but chuckle. "When will I see you?"

"We should make it there tomorrow afternoon," his brother told him.

"Thanks, bro."

After chatting a few more minutes, Deacon hung up. He found the campground, reserving half a dozen sites at the very back, since he didn't know how many would be coming. Then he started walking some more. Deacon had a part to buy and a mate to track.

ABOUT THE AUTHOR

Charlie started writing fantasy when she was eight, and after stumbling onto her first erotic romance at age nineteen, she realized her true calling. She now focuses on writing gay erotic romance, normally of the paranormal variety, with heroes of all kinds. With the help and support of her husband, Charlie finally fulfilled one of her life-long goals . . . move to acreage with her horses. You can often find her curled up with her laptop and a cup of tea or glass of wine, creating her next adventure. Charlie enjoys exploring the mountains of her new Oregon home on horseback, 4-wheeler, or motorcycle.

She can be reached at ch.richards2010@yahoo.com
Or visit her at www.charlie-richards.com

www.ingramcontent.com/pod-product-compliance
Lightning Source LLC
Chambersburg PA
CBHW070222140626
46555CB00018B/1155